"Is it the script?" Holly blurted. "I knew it. You don't like the script."

"That's not it at all." Nick reached for her hand, remembering that night on the dock when their roles were reversed and he was the one unsure of his future, needing her encouragement. "I do know a good script when I read one. And yours is good. Better than good."

"If the script's not the problem, then what is?"

Damn, he could get lost in those deep green eyes. "You've heard the expression 'actions speak louder than words,' right?"

"Of course, but I don't see what that has to do with—"

"Good." And in a move of either sheer genius or monumental stupidity, he leaned in and kissed her long and hard.

Blaze

Dear Reader,

Hi. My name is Regina. And I'm a theater geek.

On stage. Backstage. In the audience. Since I was ten years old I've been captivated by all aspects of theater. So when I decided to write a romance novel (my first!), what better place to set it than the wild, wacky, wonderful—and oh-so-sexy—world of Broadway.

At a Broadway audition, Hollywood star Nick Damone doesn't expect to find Holly Nelson, the one person who saw past his dumb jock routine in high school and encouraged him to pursue his acting dream. Holly's just as surprised. She's trying to prove herself as a playwright and get back on her feet after her messy divorce. And Nick's one tall, dark and dangerous distraction.

There's nothing like a good reunion romance, and this couple had the keys of my laptop burning up from their first encounter. But they're both damaged, touched by an issue I see all too often in my work as a senior assistant state's attorney—domestic violence. Getting them past their wounds to their own happy ending was a worthwhile challenge.

I love hearing from readers. You can find me on Facebook, www.facebook.com/reginakyleauthor, and on Twitter, @Regina_Kyle1. And keep an eye out for Holly's brother, Gabe, and her best friend, Devin. Their story is coming soon!

Until next time,

Regina

Triple Threat

—

Regina Kyle

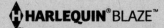

Recycling programs
for this product may
not exist in your area.

ISBN-13: 978-0-373-79822-3

TRIPLE THREAT

Printed in U.S.A.

ABOUT THE AUTHOR

Regina Kyle knew she was destined to be an author when she won a writing contest at age eight with a touching tale about a squirrel and a nut pie. By day, she writes dry legal briefs, representing the state in criminal appeals. At night, she writes steamy romance with heart and humor. A lover of all things theatrical, Regina lives on the Connecticut shoreline with her husband, teenage daughter and two melodramatic cats. When she's not writing, she's most likely singing, reading, cooking or watching bad reality television. You can find her on Facebook, www.facebook.com/reginakyleauthor, and follow @Regina_Kyle1 on Twitter.

For Dad, who always made sure my feet were planted firmly on the ground.

And Mom, who gave me wings to fly.

1

"ARE YOU OUT of your goddamn mind?" Nick Damone threw the script down on his agent's desk. To his credit, Garrett Chandler didn't flinch, most likely because he'd dealt with more than his fair share of temperamental clients. Not that Nick was temperamental. He had every right to be pissed. "Even if I wanted to play an adulterous, wife-beating scumbag—which I don't—there's absolutely no way the studio's going to go for it."

"Leave Eclipse to me. You've made them a midsize mint playing Trent Savage." Garrett sank into his butter-leather chair. "Besides, you said you wanted to get out of L.A. for a few months. So do it. Get back to your theater roots. Break free from your on-screen persona and try something edgy."

"Yeah." Nick was tired of the backstabbers and boot-lickers who were the bedrock of Hollywood society. Spent from the acrobatics of embracing fame but avoiding scandal. And at thirty-three, his days as action hero Trent Savage were numbered, and with it his livelihood unless he expanded. Denzel starred in action, drama, comedy. Won an Oscar in his thirties, another in his forties, and kept getting nominated every year or two. Robert Downey Jr. was buried in awards and prime projects, with first re-fusal on scripts that would make Nick weep on cue. If he wanted his career to have legs like that, he needed to be more than Trent Savage.

But there was edgy and there was diving off cliffs. Onto jagged rocks, at low tide, in front of a live audience. Eight times a week.

"Trust me, Nick. I didn't get you this far by pulling advice out of my ass. This role is gold. I'm talking Tony-worthy." Garrett motioned for Nick to sit in one of the webbed chairs opposite the wide mahogany desk and pushed the script toward him. "Dig into this again. I think you'll see it's everything you're looking for."

Nick sat, stretching his long legs and crossing them at the ankles. The flight from Hong Kong, where his latest picture just wrapped, had been long and damn uncomfortable. Even first class was no place for a guy of six foot four. All he wanted now was a thick steak, a hot shower and a good night's sleep. All of which he'd get after he won this argument with his worthless agent, who, unfortunately, also happened to be the closest he had to a best friend. He tended to keep people at arm's length, where they couldn't mess with his head. Or his heart.

"What do we know about this playwright?" He traced the words on the script cover, his brain taking a moment to decipher the jumbled letters. *The Lesser Vessel* by H. N. Ryan.

"Not much," Garrett admitted. "She's new. Her bio's pretty sketchy—went to Wesleyan, a few plays off-off-Broadway that closed early. But Ted and Judith say her talent is once a generation. They optioned this play before it was even finished. Coming from two of the hottest producers on Broadway, that's a pretty big endorsement."

"She?" Nick leaned forward in his chair. Spousal abuse was a hot-button topic after a spate of recent celebrity arrests, but the writing hadn't felt like an "issue" play, which—shoot him for saying so—made him assume it was written by a man.

He wouldn't admit it to Garrett, but he'd read the whole gut-wrenching story on the plane—instead of sleeping. The author had gotten into his head, and to find out the guy who spoke to him was a woman was…disconcerting.

What Garrett didn't know—what almost no one knew—was that domestic violence had been a part of Nick's daily existence for years. It still reared its ugly head every time his mom visited him, or when he talked to her on the phone. Affected him most on those rare occasions when he contemplated going home to confront his father.

He'd kept his distance, though, because he didn't trust either of them to control their rage. His mother suffered enough already. She didn't need the two of them beating each other to a pulp.

"A woman," he said again.

"Down, boy. She's not your type."

Nick didn't bother correcting Garrett's perception of him as a skirt-chasing man whore. He'd given up fighting that image. In reality, he was more of a serial monogamist, but he'd learned the hard way that it wasn't worth bucking the Hollywood machine. The press, the studio—hell, even Garrett—were happy to exploit his image as a ladies' man, truth be damned. Nothing he could do or say was going to change that. "How do you know she's not my type?"

"According to Ted, she's short, smart and sweet. That's three strikes against her in your book."

"Hey," Nick protested with a wry smile. "The women I date are sweet." Tall, leggy and vapid, sure. But sweet. He wasn't looking for a lifetime commitment. If watching his parents hadn't been enough to sour him on marriage, then dealing with the liars and cheaters in Hollywood for the past ten years had put the nail in that coffin.

Love would have to wait a very long time to catch Nick.

"I'm not kidding." Unlike Nick, Garrett wasn't smiling. "This one's off-limits. She's a serious author, not one of your blonde bimbos."

"Whatever." Garrett's threat was meaningless for one simple reason: Nick wasn't doing this play. Final answer. Game over.

Exhaustion invading like crystalline Ambien, he closed his eyes and rested his head against the back of the chair. He needed to come up with a new plan of attack or he'd find himself in a rehearsal room in Chelsea. "So the writer's legit and the play's the real deal. But why the bastard ex-husband? What about the cop?"

Garrett shook his head. "Pussy part. Besides, it's already been offered and accepted."

Nick snapped to attention. "Who?"

Garrett shuffled through some papers, doing a shit job of stalling. They both spoke fluent body language, and Nick could tell he wasn't going to like Garrett's answer. "Malcolm Justice."

"You can't be serious." It was Nick's turn to push the script back across the desk. "I wouldn't play opposite that goddamn lightweight to save my career. Even if he was the asshole ex-husband and I got to beat on his pretty-boy face every night."

"Get over it, Nick. You're Trent Savage. He's not, even if he claims he'd have been the better choice. His fans' bitching and moaning on those stupid message boards is just sour grapes."

"What about the fact that people will see me as a wife beater? Stop me in Starbucks to berate me…" The most important of those people being his mom. If she managed to sneak away from his father long enough to catch the show, she'd probably watch the whole thing from between her fingers, experiencing every blow. Stage an intervention to curb his violent tendencies. Definitely cry. A lot.

"That's the price of being an artist." Garrett poured another drink, handed it to Nick and stared out at his fortieth-floor glass-plated view.

"Some artist." Nick took a sip. He'd wondered when Garrett would get around to sharing the Maker's Mark. "I've spent the past six years playing a globe-trotting, womanizing fortune hunter. Not exactly Shakespeare."

Hell, he wasn't even sure if what he did could be considered acting anymore. And now his own agent wanted to serve him up as fodder for critics like that jerk at the *Times,* the one who made no secret of his disgust for what he called Broadway's "star worship."

As much as Nick hated to admit it, this whole thing scared him. It had been years since he'd been onstage. He figured he'd pick up where he left off before heading west, at some obscure way-off-Broadway theater where he could flop without risking career suicide.

Nick took another sip of bourbon. It scorched a warm trail down his throat, but not even that familiar, normally reassuring sensation could help him shake the feeling that he was in way over his head. Broadway? Who the fuck was he kidding?

"What's that motto you're always repeating?" Garrett's tone was mocking. "'Be beautiful, be brilliant'?"

"Be bold. Be brave." The words jolted him back almost fifteen years to a lakeside dock and the girl who'd first said them and changed his life.

Holly Nelson. He wondered if she remembered that night at the cast party as vividly as he did. The breeze ruffling her wavy brown hair. Her hand, warm and insistent on his arm, urging him to dream big. Her wide, bottle-green eyes seeing him completely, as weird as that sounded. Not just who he was but who he could become.

No, she probably didn't remember any of that. Probably didn't remember their kiss, either, although it was imprinted in his brain. He'd known she was inexperienced, and he'd meant it to be innocent, a thank-you for telling him what he needed to hear. But the second his lips met hers, all thoughts of innocence had disintegrated. She'd melted in his arms like butter, soft and pliant. He'd closed his eyes against the rush of pleasure as her mouth opened to him and her hands fluttered up to stroke his chest through his T-shirt. He'd been so far gone he hadn't seen Jessie Pagano sauntering across the lawn to interrupt them until it was too late. Lost camera, his ass.

While he'd thought about Holly over the years more than he cared to admit, Nick hadn't kept track of her. He owed her for kick-starting his acting career, but it would be presumptuous to track her down. He imagined her back home in suburban Stockton, married to a high school gym teacher, with kids she kissed and praised all day. *What would she think of this whole Broadway thing?*

"You okay, buddy?"

Garrett's voice brought Nick back to the present. He downed the rest of his bourbon and wiped his mouth, nodding. "Fine."

"So you'll meet with the production team?"

Shit. "Where and when?"

"New York." Garrett paused to finish off his drink, and once again Nick knew what followed was going to be bad news. "Tomorrow afternoon."

"No way. I just got off a goddamn plane. Can't it wait a few days?"

"No can do. Casting was supposed to be finished last week but they held off, waiting for you to return stateside. Seems someone over there's got a real hard-on for you in this part."

"Jesus Christ."

"You said it, brother. That's why I booked both of us on the red-eye."

"Pretty sure of yourself, aren't you?"

"Sure this part will catapult you to the next level, if that's what you mean. Rumor has it Spielberg's shopping a Joe DiMaggio biopic. You'd be a great fit for the title role, and this play is just the thing to put you on his radar."

Damn. Nick would give his left nut to work with Spielberg. And Joltin' Joe was a national hero.

He slumped over and ran a hand through his hair. It was a foregone conclusion Garrett would win this battle, but he felt compelled to take one last stand. "I'm starving, exhausted and in serious need of a shower."

"No problem." Garrett crossed the room and grabbed his jacket off a coatrack. "We've got just enough time to get to your place for you to clean up and pack. You can sleep and eat on the plane."

"What about you?"

Garrett picked up an overnight bag from behind the coatrack. "All set."

"Cocky son of a bitch." Nick grinned in spite of himself.

"That's why I make the big bucks." Garrett swung open his office door and strode out.

Nick grabbed the script and followed him. There was no way he'd be sleeping on the plane. If he was auditioning for the powers that be, he intended to be prepared. He needed to reread the play at least twice, break down specific scenes, write a character bio... Not easy tasks given his dyslexia.

"This better be worth it." He slipped on a pair of Oakley sunglasses. "Or I'll be in the market for a new agent. And a new best friend."

2

HOLLY RYAN TURNED her head, trying to catch a glimpse of her backside in the black linen dress pants, and scowled. "They're too tight. I don't know what was wrong with what I had on."

"These old things?" Her sister Noelle nudged the pale pink button-down and khakis lying in a heap on the floor with her foot. "Please. They made you look like a hausfrau. Now you've got a waist. And an ass. And how about those boobs? I feel like I've just unearthed Atlantis."

"Which brings us to our next problem." Holly toyed with the plunging neckline of the silk blouse, another loaner from her baby sister, who, at twenty-six, was a full-blown fashionista. "Isn't this a little…"

"Flattering? Attractive? Eye-catching?"

"I was thinking more like revealing. Inappropriate. Slutty."

Noelle put a hand to her heart and staggered as if she'd been shot. "You wound me, sis. That's my lucky Marc Jacobs chemise. I wore it to my first opening night party. *Giselle.*"

Holly trudged to her bed and collapsed. All this primping was exhausting. First, Noelle had insisted on styling Holly's notoriously stick-straight hair. Then she'd spent an hour applying just the right amount of makeup. And now she was forcing Holly to play dress-up. It was like senior prom all over again, when twelve-year-old Noelle had schooled Holly on all the "girlie girl" things that were still so foreign to her.

"It's not that I'm not grateful for all your effort, Noe." Holly flopped onto her back, bouncing a bit on the too-firm mattress. "I just don't understand why it's necessary."

"First of all," Noelle began, sitting on the bed next to her and holding up one finger in a gesture that said a list of reasons was forthcoming, "you deserve a little pampering after the past couple of years you've had. Consider it your reward for dumping that bottom-feeder, Clark."

"Can't argue with that." Holly pushed up onto her elbows. Her sister didn't know the half of it. No one did except the police and a handful of medical professionals.

"And second—" Noelle held up another finger "—you're a big-time playwright now. You've got to look the part."

Holly rolled her eyes. "I'm nowhere near big-time."

Noelle gave her a playful smack upside the head. "Wake up and smell the success, girl! Your play's headed for Broadway. With at least one, maybe even two major movie stars. I'd call that big-time."

She had a point. But Holly had a hard time thinking of herself as anything other than the perennial screw-up in a family of overachievers. Her three younger siblings had each climbed their career mountains and planted their flags on top, wisely ignoring the example of their hopeless older sister. Holly had had more jobs than hairstyles, from substitute teaching to bartending to dog walking. It had become something of a family joke, guessing what she'd "explore" next. "Holly's follies," they called them.

The "follies" stopped a couple of years into her five-year marriage, when Clark had decided he wanted her at home, happy to greet him at the door each evening with a gin and tonic in her hand and dinner on the table. Always game, Holly had tried the new role.

Massive mistake.

Domestic goddesshood evaded her, at least in Clark's estimation. Dinner was always overdone or underdone, the toilets never sufficiently shiny, his shirts never starched enough. Her saving grace—what made the debacle bearable—was an article in a women's magazine about the benefits of journaling.

And thus H. N. Ryan, author, was born.

"I'll believe it when I see the marquee go up." A healthy chunk of her still doubted that would ever happen. There were too many ways things could crash and burn in high def. "Until then…"

"Honestly, Holls." Noelle pushed a strand of long blond hair, so different from Holly's, behind one ear. "You worry too much. You said the producers signed Malcolm Justice to play the cop, right?"

Holly nodded and sat up fully.

"And this new guy? The one who's reading for you today?" Noelle turned away from Holly to the selection of shoes she had lined up at the foot of the bed. Holly groaned inwardly. Not one of them had a heel less than four inches.

"No clue. All Ethan would say is that he's a grade-A film star and major heartthrob."

Which was strange, Holly thought. They never kept secrets. Ethan Phelps had been her best friend since their freshman year at Wesleyan when she'd helped him conquer Chaucer and Dickens. He'd rewarded her with the irritating nickname "Hollypop," a name he unfortunately still insisted on using.

When her agent told her that *The Lesser Vessel* had been optioned for Broadway, her second thought—after *Are you drunk?*—was whether they'd consider Ethan to direct. Fortunately, the producers loved his regional-theater work.

"What if it's George Clooney?" Noelle froze, her ballerina's feet in a pensive third position. "Or Tom Cruise?"

Holly shook her head. "Too old. And too…Tom Cruise."

"Ooh, how about Nick Damone?" Holly almost choked on her tongue, but Noelle, who had moved on to a collection of jewelry spread across the dresser, didn't seem to notice. "You could finally do something about that crush you had on him in high school."

"What do you mean?"

"Please, Holls. Give me some credit."

"But you were *ten.*" And all this time she thought Ethan was the only one who knew. She'd confessed her long-ago crush on the now-famous movie star one night shortly after her divorce was final, an aftereffect of too many rum and Cokes.

But she'd never told anyone—not even Ethan—that she was the one who'd convinced Nick to ditch his football scholarship and go to New York, or that he'd kissed her that night at the cast party. Her first kiss, and no other boy had come close to making her heart race and her insides quiver the way Nick had. Of course, that magic moment had ended all too soon when Jessie Pagano came looking for her camera. *Right.* With one crook of her perfectly manicured finger she'd lured Nick away like a pied piper in do-me heels.

Ethan and Noelle would have never let her live that down. So Holly resorted to the safest tactic she knew: deny, deny, deny. "What did you know about crushes? I do not, *did not,* have a thing for Nick Damone."

"Then why are you blushing like a virgin at a strip club?"

"I am not blushing!" Holly covered her face with her

hands. *Crap.* Her sister was right. Her cheeks felt as hot as the pottery kiln she'd bought during what her family referred to as her "terra-cotta phase."

"It's no big deal. I've got a thing for Ryan Gosling. Seven minutes alone with that man in a closet and I'd definitely be in heaven."

"Thing or no thing, it doesn't matter. According to *Variety,* Nick's still in Hong Kong shooting the new Trent Savage flick."

"Well, whoever your mystery movie star is, you need these to close the deal." Noelle picked up a pair of silver peep-toe sling backs and dangled them from her fingertips. "Christian Louboutin."

As if that meant anything to Holly. "No way."

Noelle smiled with far more wicked intent than any woman wanted to see in her baby sister. "You have to. Guys think they're sexy."

"I'm shooting for professional, not sexy." Holly went to her closet and pulled out a pair of simple, low black pumps, the only pair of heels she owned. Practically new, since she barely wore them. She shoved them on. "These are more my speed."

"Oh, well. Can't blame a girl for trying." Noelle tossed the Louboutins aside, bent down and rummaged around in her Gucci carry-on, pulling out a thick black belt. "Just a couple of final touches."

She fastened the belt around Holly's waist, centering the large oval buckle, then handed her a pair of garnet studs and a matching necklace from the bureau. "Now you're ready to kick ass and take names. And if it's—please, God—Ryan Gosling, call me and don't let him out the door before I get there."

Half an hour later, Holly paced outside the Film Center Building on Ninth Avenue, hitting Redial on her cell phone again. And again. And again. "Come on, Ethan! Pick up, dammit! Where are you?"

"Right behind you, Hollypop."

She jumped and spun around, teetering until Ethan grabbed her by the arms and steadied her. "Ethan, you scared me! And you're late. And you know I hate that nickname."

He gave her a kiss on the forehead and released her. "Aw, don't be mad, Holls. That frown doesn't go with the fabulous getup you're rocking."

"You know I can never stay mad at you." She returned his kiss with a peck on the cheek.

A trace of something like regret flashed across Ethan's face. "Tell me that again in a few minutes," he muttered, then changed the subject. "Nice duds. Did you take my advice and call Noelle?"

She nodded and glanced down at the hint of cleavage just visible in the folds of her sister's blouse. "You think it's okay? Not too much?"

"Better than okay. And definitely not too much." He took her elbow and steered her to the door. "Now, let's get this party started."

They whipped past the doorman, through the lobby and into the elevator. "What's with all the mystery, Ethan? You planning on telling me who's upstairs waiting for us?"

"You'll find out soon enough." He shuffled his feet and punched the button for the fourteenth floor twice more.

"Why so nervous? We've been auditioning big-name stars for weeks. Even hired one of them."

"Not like this." The elevator dinged and Ethan motioned for her to precede him out. "Let's just say if we sign this guy it'll be the biggest news to hit the Great White Way since Hugh Jackman and Daniel Craig in *A Steady Rain*."

Holly paused at the familiar door to the offices of

Broadway producers Ted and Judith Aaronson. "I'd faint if it was one of them."

"It's not. But you just might faint anyway."

"Promise you'll catch me if I do." She reached for the doorknob, but he stopped her with a hand on her wrist, his soft gray eyes serious.

"Sure, if you promise me something in return."

"As long as it doesn't involve anything illegal, immoral or fattening."

"Whatever happens in there, promise you won't hate me."

"Hate you? Why would I hate you?" She shook his hand off, her stomach knotting up like a ball of yarn. "You're freaking me out, Ethan. Who's waiting for us in there? The pope? Jimmy Hoffa? My ex-mother-in-law?"

Before he could answer, the door fell open with a *whoosh*.

"Here they are!" Ted opened the door wider, ushering them inside. "Our esteemed writer and director." He brought them into a conference room where Judith and several others were seated in tapestry chairs around an enormous walnut table. One man stood apart, his back to the door, apparently engrossed in one of the framed photos of the New York skyline that dotted the walls. Black hair curled over the collar of his cream-colored dress shirt, which hugged his broad shoulders and displayed strong forearms beneath rolled-up sleeves.

No. It couldn't be him. He was supposed to be on a movie set overseas...

"Holly Ryan, Ethan Phelps," Ted boomed, earning him a stern look from his wife. He either ignored or missed it and continued, not lowering his voice one decibel. "Say hello to our new star, straight from the silver screen."

The man turned and Holly knew from his slack-jawed expression that he was as shocked as she was.

Nick.

He moved toward her like a tidal wave of gorgeous in an ocean of ohmigod. "It's been a long time, Holly." Tall, dark and to-die-for, he held out his hand. His voice, deep and rough, made her breath catch and her nipples tighten. She crossed her arms in front of her chest to hide her unfortunate and completely involuntary reaction to the man who had starred in her erotic dreams since—well, since she'd been old enough to have erotic dreams.

"Nick. I thought you were in Hong Kong." She stood, feet planted, afraid if she got any nearer to him she'd dissolve into a pool of fiery, lust-ridden goo.

"Been keeping up with me?" He dropped his hand when she didn't move to take it, slipping it casually into the front pocket of his jeans. "I'm flattered."

"It's hard not to. You're everywhere."

"Ethan didn't tell you?" Ted stepped in, smile lines further crinkling his already wrinkled face, and clapped the director on the shoulder. Ethan gave him a warning glare, but the older man, either truly oblivious or deliberately ignorant, ran a hand through his salt-and-pepper hair and continued, "He insisted we see Nick for this role, that he'd be perfect as our modern-day Stanley Kowalski. Even convinced us to put off casting until he finished shooting."

"Perfect," Holly echoed, her blood closely approaching the boiling point.

A bead of sweat trickled down Ethan's forehead and his Adam's apple did a nervous dance in his throat. "Surprise."

3

NICK OWED ETHAN PHELPS one hell of an expensive bottle of Scotch. He didn't know why, but thanks to Phelps he was face-to-face with Holly Nelson. His teenage fantasy, all grown up.

Unfortunately, his teenage fantasy didn't seem to want anything to do with him. Instead, she dragged the director into a corner where they conversed in hushed tones. Nick caught comments like "what the hell were you thinking" and "not in this lifetime."

Looked as if he wasn't the only one knocked for a loop by their little reunion. Too bad he was the only one happy about it.

Nick took advantage of Holly's distraction to look at her. Really look at her. She was dressed a bit more provocatively than she used to. Wearing more makeup, too. And her hair was different, all spiky and brushed to one side.

The soft, sweet curve of her breasts peeked from the low-cut neckline of her blouse, but under the designer clothes and makeup was the girl he remembered. She'd filled out, of course, and in all the right places. But it was still Holly, with those piercing green eyes.

She stabbed a finger at Ethan's chest to make some particularly passionate point. The movement thrust those delectable breasts out farther.

Oh, yeah. She'd grown up, all right. But what was she doing here? She seemed awfully familiar with the director. His assistant, maybe?

He eased himself into a chair and reached for the pitcher of ice water at the center of the table. As he did, the cover of his script, and the name of the author inscribed across it, caught his eye.

H. N. Ryan.

And then it hit him. Ted had introduced her as Holly Ryan. Holly was the playwright. Holly Nelson Ryan.

"Why don't we all sit down and get things rolling." Judith's sharp Brooklyn accent jolted Nick back to the conference room. "Colleen," she continued, turning to a pretty blonde lurking by the door, "why don't you get Holly a copy of the script. She can—"

"Read the role of the wife," Ted finished for Judith. She frowned and pulled out a chair at the end of the table, as far from her husband as possible. "Wonderful."

"Of course." The blonde disappeared momentarily, then returned with script in hand. "Here you are, Mrs. Ryan."

Shit.

She was married. Sweet little Holly Nelson, the object of some of his hottest adolescent fantasies, was Mrs. Holly Ryan. Wife. Playwright. Maybe even mother.

Tony award and Spielberg film be damned, there was no way in hell he could work side by side with Holly for months on end, all the while silently lusting after her. *Or maybe not so silently,* he thought. He watched her smile as she took the script from Colleen, the tip of her tongue darting out to swipe her lips. He bit back a groan at the unconsciously erotic gesture.

This play already had two strikes against it as far as Nick was concerned. He hadn't been onstage in years, and he had dyslexia. He'd need to be completely focused to pull it off. No distractions. And Holly had distraction written all over her—untouchable, unattainable distraction.

He eyed Garrett sitting next to him. There was no way around it. His agent would have to learn to live with the disappointment.

"Nick." Ethan took a seat across the table. "I understand you and Holly go way back." Ethan winced and frowned at Holly in the chair to his left. She returned his grimace with a smirk, and Nick was pretty sure she'd just kicked the director under the table. What exactly was their relationship, anyway?

"Yes. We grew up together in Stockton, Connecticut." *The big dumb jock and the cute little honors student.* "Just outside New Haven."

"Well," Ted said. "That makes this even better." He paused and looked around the table for dramatic effect. "Let's start with act one, scene two, the argument at the dinner table."

Holly's face reddened and she ducked her head, frantically turning the pages of her script. "Of course."

Fuck. Getting out of this was going to be harder than he thought.

"Actually, Ted, I—"

"Nick," Garrett interrupted, glaring at him, "would be happy to—"

"What I'm trying to say," Nick said, glaring right back, "is that I'm sorry I wasted your time, but I don't think this project's right for me." He stood, leaving his script on the table, and risked one last glance at Holly. Damn, she looked fine. Good enough to eat, starting with those lush lips and working his way down, inch by glorious inch. "It was nice seeing you, Holly. Good luck with…everything."

He strode to the door, barely registering Garrett's song and dance of apologies in the wake of his startling announcement. The guy was a hustler, he'd give him that. But no amount of hustling was going to change Nick's mind. He'd just have to find another way to redefine his career and impress Spielberg. One that didn't involve the very diverting—and very married—Holly Nelson Ryan.

"NO, NO, A THOUSAND times no!" Holly paced the length of the conference room, now empty except for her and Ethan.

He leaned forward in his chair, elbows on the table, hands steepled under his chin. "You heard Ted and Judith. No Nick, no show. They've got a group of private investors lined up, but before they cough up any dough they want to see Nick signed on the dotted line."

"Why Nick?" Holly whined, still pacing. "Can't we just get another star?"

Ethan lifted a shoulder. "Guess my sales pitch was a little too convincing."

"Then why me?" She couldn't do what they were asking. It was too risky. "Why can't you persuade him? You brought him here. Or Ted? Or Judith?"

Ethan raised an eyebrow. "Because Nick wasn't looking at me or Ted or Judith like he wanted to throw us onto the conference table and go all caveman."

That stopped Holly in her tracks. "You are majorly delusional. He barely glanced my way."

She, on the other hand, hadn't been able to take her eyes off him from the moment she'd walked in the door. His presence had seemed to take up the whole room. She'd seen one or two of his movies. Okay, she'd seen them all multiple times, and owned the DVDs. But that hadn't even remotely prepared her for Nick Damone, live, in person and sexy as sin.

He had those mocha eyes, as dark and smoky as she remembered but even more intense, more penetrating.

When she was able to break free from their strange, hypnotic spell, her addled brain registered a scraggly beard and moustache, probably grown for his last picture. Sprinkled with silver, they highlighted his strong jaw, making him appear, if possible, even more masculine. One lock of hair had flopped temptingly across his brow, and she'd longed to reach up—way up, given the difference in their heights—and brush it back.

And that was just his face. As for his body...

Yowza.

He'd always been tall, but the lean, athletic boy she remembered had filled out and become a hard, muscular, mouthwateringly beautiful man. His dress shirt clung to his biceps and broad chest, falling loosely over what she knew must be washboard abs. Well-worn jeans rode low on his hips and molded to his powerful thighs and taut, trim butt. She'd tried—but failed—not to notice how they cupped certain other areas as well.

Ethan pushed his chair back from the table and walked over to her. "You're wrong, Holls. The sexual tension in the room was off the charts from the second you laid eyes on each other. And it definitely wasn't a one-way street."

"So what are you saying? You want me to seduce him into taking the part?"

"No. Of course not." He put a hand on her shoulder. "We want you to talk to him. Just talk. It's obvious you two have some sort of connection. He'll listen to you."

She shook his hand off. "I can't believe you're asking me to do this. After the way you sandbagged me! I should be mad at you, you know. Strike that. I *am* mad at you."

"You know if I had told you it was Nick, you would have flipped out."

"I would not have."

"Then why are you flipping out now? So you had a

crush on him as a kid. Big deal. It's ancient history." He paused, his eyes narrowing. "Unless there's something you're not telling me…"

"No." She resisted the urge to check her nose to see if it was growing after that whopper. "I just don't know what I can say that will convince him to take this part."

"Tell him what you told me when I came on as director. That you wrote *The Lesser Vessel* because you want to help other women in the same situation find the courage to get the hell out."

Courage. Hah. What did she know about courage?

"Please, Holls," Ethan begged, blessedly interrupting the dark turn of her thoughts. "It's our best chance of getting this show off the ground."

"You want me to admit he'd be playing my ex-husband? Blurt out my whole sordid life story?"

"Okay, skip that part. But let him know how important the message of this show is. Not just to you but to the whole production team. We believe in you *and* your play, Holly. He will, too, if you give him the chance."

"Well, when you put it that way…" She took a deep breath, then blew it out loudly through pursed lips. "Fine. I'll go."

"And if the subject of your past relationship comes up…"

"I told you. There's nothing to discuss. There is—was—no relationship." Holly made her way to the door. "I'm beginning to regret this already. Remind me again why you can't join me on this little errand?"

"It's Jean-Michel's birthday. He'll kill me if I'm late for the celebratory dinner I supposedly planned for him that was really all his doing. Besides," he teased, his eyes sparkling and one corner of his mouth turned up mischievously, "you know what they say."

"What?"

"Three's a crowd."

She rolled her eyes and turned to leave.

"Holly, wait. I know I might sound flip, but this is serious." His words—and his tone—made her pause with one hand on the doorknob. "Clark's a first-class jack hole who deserves to be put in front of a firing squad. But he's your past. It's time to start thinking about your future."

He crossed to her and squeezed her shoulder. "You've been alone long enough. And you might never get a chance like this again. Don't you owe it to yourself to figure out what this crazy chemistry between you and *People*'s Sexiest Man Alive is about?"

She turned to him, tears threatening to spill over. "Damn you, Ethan. How am I supposed to stay mad at you when you say stuff like that?"

"You're not." He smiled, flashing a solitary dimple on his left cheek. "Just don't let it get around. I've got a reputation as a tough guy to uphold."

"If you say so." With a final squeeze, she stepped out of his embrace and wiped her eyes.

"He's staying at the Marquis." He handed her a business card with the hotel's address scrawled on the back. "Room 1008."

4

HOLLY CHECKED THE card in her hand once more before knocking on the door: 1008. Good. She was in the right place.

Or the wrong place.

She exhaled loudly, shaking off her doubts, and knocked. She was there to talk. Just talk. She was a grown woman, for goodness' sake, not a hormonal teenager. She wasn't going to be distracted by...

The door swung open and any thoughts of talking—not to mention her ability to talk at all—deserted her. Nick stood framed in the doorway, a skimpy hotel towel wrapped loosely around his waist. He was still damp from the shower, those washboard abs she'd speculated about earlier on full display.

So much for not being distracted.

He leaned against the doorjamb. "You're not Garrett."

"I-I'm sorry for barging in like this," she stammered, finding her voice and trying not to ogle the firm, wet flesh of his bare chest and arms. She swallowed. Hard. "Guess I should have called first."

"No, it's...it's fine." He stepped back to wave her in and the towel slipped to his hips, giving her a view of the trail of fine, dark hair leading from his navel to the promised land. She licked her lips. "Just give me a minute to put something on."

Don't bother on my account.

"You can wait in here." He led her into a sunken living room, complete with not one but two plush sofas and a Steinway piano, and disappeared into what she presumed was the bedroom.

Heart pounding, she wandered to the piano, setting her clutch down and fingering the keys. "Do you play?" she called out, desperate to fill the awkward silence.

"No," he answered from the other room. "Garrett insisted I have the Presidential Suite. I'd have been happy in a regular guest room, but Garrett's a top-of-the-line kind of guy."

She left the piano and moved to a wall of windows overlooking Times Square, absorbing the spectacular view. Almost as spectacular as the view of Nick's butt in that towel…

"He can be a jerk when things aren't going his way, but I trust him," Nick continued as he came back into the lounge. "He's got my best interests at heart."

Holly turned from the window to face him. *Holy hotness, Batman!* He'd zipped himself into another pair of jeans, just as snug as the ones he'd had on before but even more faded and ripped at one knee, and was buttoning a light gray sports shirt. He padded toward her on bare feet with the easy grace of a man comfortable in his own skin.

If she could bottle that self-confidence and sell it, she'd be a millionaire. Or maybe he could give her lessons.…

He lowered himself onto one of the couches and motioned for her to join him, but she shook her head. She could barely think straight with him all the way across the room. She didn't stand a chance up close and personal.

"So what brings you here?" he asked. "Ted and Judith send you to change my mind?"

She wanted to tell him the truth. Really, she did. But when she opened her mouth, something entirely different came out. "Not exactly. I, uh, wanted to apologize. For my behavior today in the conference room. I was inexcusably rude."

He glanced at the platinum Rolex on his left wrist. "You came all the way across town at rush hour to apologize?" He leaned back and crossed his arms behind his head. His biceps bulged beneath his shirt sleeves.

Her mouth went dry. Good Lord, the man was unsettling. "Well, yes. It was such a surprise, seeing you. I reacted...poorly."

Right. And Shakespeare just scribbled down a few poems and plays.

"So you don't want to strong-arm me into auditioning?" He fixed her with a piercing stare that she did her best to meet head-on.

"Do I look like I could strong-arm anyone?"

"You look..." the same eyes that had just tried to intimidate her with their intensity raked her up and down, leaving her tingling and breathless "...stunning."

She shivered and stepped back, leaning against the piano for support. One word—one look—and she was ready to throw off her clothes and beg him to do her in every yoga position imaginable.

This was wrong. All wrong. She never should have come. How did Ted and Judith and especially Ethan expect her to keep her pants on when faced with a force of nature like Nick? She wasn't exactly a femme fatale. More like a poor man's Cinderella, all dressed up for the ball, waiting for the stroke of midnight to reveal her as a complete fraud. Certainly no match for the charm and sophistication of Nick Damone.

"Thanks." She wiped her clammy hands on the legs of her linen pants. "But all this—" she indicated her new hairdo, makeup and clothes "—it's not really me. I'm more of a just-rolled-out-of-bed, jeans-and-T-shirt kind of gal. Nothing like the glamorous women you're always photographed with."

His smile put her in mind of a wolf eyeing a sheep before the kill. "Exactly."

She wasn't sure what he meant by that and she wasn't dumb—or brave—enough to stick around and find out. "I've taken up enough of your time." She snatched her clutch off the piano. "Thanks for flying all the way out here to meet with us. I'm sorry it was all for nothing...."

"What does your husband think about you coming to my hotel room like this?"

"My...what?"

"You know, your husband. Mr. Ryan. The man you married." He sat straighter, his eyes flashing. "Does he know you're here?"

The last thing she wanted to discuss with Nick was her pathetic excuse for a husband. But she supposed she owed Nick the truth—or part of it.

"I don't have a husband. Not anymore. I'm divorced."

HOT DAMN!

Nick knew his reaction was wrong. No matter the circumstances, divorce wasn't something to celebrate. But his head couldn't reason with his heart, which was doing a little happy dance.

She. Wasn't. Married.

Lusting after her from afar would have been torture.

But now she was free. Fair game. They could work *and* play together.

Warning bells went off in the back of his head. *She's a forever kind of girl, Damone. And you don't do forever. In fact, you don't do relationships. Period.*

But his happy-dancing heart—or maybe the dancing was coming from somewhere a bit farther south—drowned it out. There was no way he was passing up the second chance given to him by God, or fate, or whatever cosmic force had brought them together again.

Plus, if anyone could help him get past his learning disability and claim this role, it was her. Hell, she'd written the damn thing. She'd know the characters inside out. Plus, she was the smartest person he'd ever met. With her help, he'd wow Spielberg and everyone else in Hollywood who doubted his acting chops.

Nick smoothed down the front of his shirt and stretched one arm along the back of the couch. This could turn out to be his lucky break. In more ways than one.

"I'm sorry," he said, surprised to find that a part of him really was. Not that she was available, but that she'd had to endure the pain that always came with divorce.

She shrugged, the hint of a smile playing around her lips. "I'm not."

"Any kids?"

As suddenly as it appeared, the trace of a smile vanished and her eyes took on a distant look. "No."

"That's good."

"Is it?" She sounded wistful.

"Divorce is hard on kids." Although he was pretty sure his childhood would have been a damn sight better—or at least more peaceful—if his parents had split up.

"I suppose." She shook her head as if to clear it, and a little of the spark crept back into her eyes. "Now that we've exhausted the subject of my failed marriage…" She started for the door.

He sank back into the sofa, crossing an ankle over one knee. "You honestly didn't come here to get me to audition?"

She froze. "Are you always this suspicious?"

He shrugged. "Occupational hazard. You haven't answered my question."

"I do want you to audition. But it's your decision, not mine."

"That's very Dr. Phil of you," he said, sounding cynical even to his own ears. "But somehow I don't think Ted and Judith share your concern for my feelings. If I were a betting man, and I am, I'd say they're trying to cash in on our friendship."

"I'm not privy to their innermost thoughts." Holly drew herself up and pursed her lips. Man, she was hot when she went all schoolteacher. "And one conversation at a high school cast party hardly constitutes a friendship."

Nick leaned forward, elbows on his knees, giving her the full force of his patented movie-star smile. "If memory serves, we did a little more than talk that night."

"Did we?"

"Need a reminder?" He braced himself to stand.

"No!" She lost her grip on the ridiculously tiny sparkly thing she seemed to think was a purse, sending it clattering to the floor. "It's been lovely catching up, but I've got another appointment." She bent to pick it up so quickly she almost fell on her sweet little backside.

Oh, yeah. She remembered that kiss. And she'd been as turned on by it as much as he had.

Unfortunately, she was also on the run, halfway to the door.

He resisted the urge to jump up and grab her, not want-

ing to scare her any more than he already had. He needed
to tone down the he-man antics if he had any hope of convincing her to stay. "Please stop."

She didn't.

"I was an ass."

She hesitated, only inches from the door and freedom.
"Now or then?"

"Both."

She turned slowly, and met his gaze head-on. "Thank
you."

"Don't go." He slid over on the sofa, making room for
her. "I'd like a chance to explain why I turned you down."
And that he'd since changed his mind.

"Now?" she asked with a smirk. "Or then?"

He winced. "Now." He definitely wanted to focus on
the present. Their present.

"I have another engagement."

"No," he said. "You don't. Hear me out, Holly."

She nodded stiffly, her already rosy cheeks deepening
to a bright scarlet, and sat on the other couch, as far away
from him as possible.

"Can I get you a drink? Or I can call room service if
you're hungry."

"No, thanks. I'm fine." She took out her cell phone and
glanced at the screen. "I can give you five minutes."

Five minutes. Okay. He had this. He took a deep breath.
"I walked out this afternoon because…" Because what?
The air thinned when she was around? He couldn't stop
picturing her under him, panting? He wanted to pummel
her ex-husband without even knowing the guy?

He stared at the place where her neck met her shoulder
and tried like hell to think of something safe. Sunshine.
Cotton candy. The box-office numbers from the last Savage picture.

"Is it the script?" she blurted. "I knew it. You don't like the script."

"That's not it at all." He got up and joined her on the other couch, breathing a sigh of relief when she didn't shift away from him. "The script is brilliant. Moving and smart without being sappy. Not at all what I expected from a play dealing with domestic violence."

She bristled and he knew he'd put his foot in his mouth. Again. "What did you expect? Some hackneyed, stereotypically pedantic melodrama?"

"To be honest, sweetheart, I don't even know what half those words mean," he joked, falling back on the dumbjock routine he'd used in school to mask his learning disability. But he grew serious when he looked into her eyes, wide and stricken, filled with uncertainty.

He reached for her hand and was reminded of that night on the dock when their roles were reversed and he was the one unsure of his future, needing her encouragement. "But I do know a good script when I read one. And yours is good. Better than good."

"If the script's not the problem, then what is?" Damn, he could get lost in those deep green eyes.

"You've heard the expression 'actions speak louder than words,' right?"

"Of course, but I don't see what that has to do with—"

"Good." And in a move of either sheer genius or monumental stupidity, he leaned in and kissed her, long and hard.

IT WAS HAPPENING AGAIN. Nick Damone was kissing her. And just like before, she couldn't resist it. Couldn't resist him. His touch, like a magnet, drawing her blood to the surface of her skin. His taste, like caramel, with a hint of Scotch.

Resist? Hell. Who was she kidding? She was responding to him like a sex-starved nympho. And while she'd admit to being sex-starved, she wasn't a nymphomaniac. Yet. But if Nick kept kissing her like that…and that…and, oh, yes, that…

Everything else vanished into the vortex of Nick's warm, hungry mouth. There was no play. No Ethan waiting for her to report on her mission. No Noelle or the rest of her family waiting to pick her up after yet another failure.

Only Nick.

Or, more specifically, Nick's mouth, hot and insistent.

She hissed and arched into him as he skimmed a hand up her rib cage to her breast, cupping it through her blouse and brushing the soft silk across her nipple with his thumb. His other hand wound its way through her hair, keeping her head at the perfect angle for his heated kiss. He licked and nibbled and sucked at her lips from corner to corner until she thought she'd pass out from pure pleasure.

"Nick," she panted when he finally paused to breathe. "I don't think…"

"That's right, sweetheart." He disentangled his hand from her hair and with one finger traced the delicate shell of her ear. "Don't think." He followed his finger with his tongue. "Just feel."

She was feeling, all right. For the first time since— well, long before her divorce—she was wild for a man. This man. The way his breath sent a current down her ear. The pricks on her skin from the scruff of his beard, lighting a path down.

Down.

And the hand on her breast… Oh, Lord. She shuddered as he teased first one, then the other, through her blouse, until her already aching nipples puckered into tight little buds.

"God…Nick." Her head fell back, giving him greater

access to the line of her neck. He drew a hot, wet trail from the sensitive spot behind her ear to the hollow at the base of her throat.

"So soft," he murmured against her skin, wrapping his arms around her. "So sweet." He pulled her closer, stroking her back until she was pressed against him so intimately she could feel every hard, solid inch of him. Especially the hard, solid inches pushing on her girl parts and making them all warm and tingly.

Her hips responded, rocking back and forth. Her hands moved, too, restless and hungry. They slid under his shirt and explored the ripped landscape of his chest and abdomen that her eyes had feasted on when he'd opened the door. Hot, hard muscle scorched her palms as her fingers threaded their way through the perfect smattering of silky, fine hair.

"Whoa, girl." He grabbed her hips, stilling her, and gave her another one of those lazy, movie-star smiles. "Keep that up and I'm going to come before either of us gets naked."

Naked. That one word sent a wave of terror through Holly. No one outside of a hospital had seen her naked since that night. That awful night when she'd told Clark she was leaving him. In the blink of an eye he'd gone from a controlling, manipulative bastard to a physically abusive one. An image of her stomach laced with angry red scars flashed through her brain. If Nick saw them…

Holly shuddered and forced herself to push away from him, creating at least a little distance between them even though his rip-cord arms still held her close. She'd been a fool to let things get this far. They had to stop. Now. Before he saw her scars and started pressing for answers she wasn't ready to give him.

"I'm sorry, Nick. I can't… We can't…"

She braced for the explosion, the anger, the name-calling and blame. That's what she would have gotten from Clark. Instead, Nick loosened his hold and let her slide to the opposite end of the couch. With that little bit of distance, the pressure that had been building inside her like a fast-rising river released.

"Don't be sorry." His lips curved into a smile, and his eyes, still dark with passion, met hers. "I'm not. Horny as hell, yeah. But not sorry."

"Thanks." She shook her head, bemused. How could he stay so cool and calm on the surface? Weren't his insides churning like hers? "I think." She started to get up, feeling shaken. "I should go now."

He stood and offered her his hand. "I'll show you out."

"My purse?" She scanned the room, her eyes finally landing on a slip of sliver poking out from under the sofa.

He bent, picked it up and walked her to the door. "Like I said earlier, it's nice seeing you." He handed her the purse with a cheeky grin. "Again."

"Same here." She squared her shoulders and opened the door, trying to regain some semblance of composure. Not easy with her outfit stuck to her flushed skin and her throat as dry as a Thanksgiving turkey. "Thanks for meeting with us. And don't worry about the play. I'm sure we'll find someone wonderful for the part."

He rested his big, beautiful frame against the wall. "I'm sure you will, sweetheart. I'm sure you will."

The door swung shut behind her, putting sex god and heart-stopper Nick Damone in her past once and for all.

Holly took a few careful steps on wobbly sea legs, then collapsed against a column. She touched her lips, still swollen from Nick's kiss, not sure whether to be relieved or disappointed.

From the other side of the door she heard a low chuckle.

Relieved, she thought, striding down the hall with re-newed determination. *Definitely relieved.*

And disappointed.

5

"THIS IS ALL your fault." Holly stabbed at a lettuce leaf and glared from Ethan to Noelle. Why had she agreed to meet them at the Westway, one of her favorite city restaurants? She couldn't scream or throw things at them without risking getting thrown out. Or worse, banned. So instead, she had to be satisfied with massacring her poor innocent gorgonzola chicken salad.

It was a poor substitute.

"You." She fixed her eyes on Noelle. "Dolling me up for him. And you." Her gaze shifted to Ethan. "Sending me to his hotel room like a lamb to the slaughter."

"Wait a minute." Noelle turned on Ethan. "You told me it was her idea to go to Nick's!"

"I never said it was Holly's idea. I said she agreed to go."

"But you made it seem like she was a willing participant." Noelle eyed her sister across the table. "She doesn't look so willing now."

"It doesn't matter whose idea it was," Holly interrupted. "What matters is that I went. And it was an unmitigated disaster."

"It couldn't have been that bad." Ethan sipped his mineral water. "Unless… Oh, my God. You slept with him, didn't you?"

"She did not! She's my sister. She doesn't put out on a first date."

"It wasn't a date," Holly pointed out.

"Even better. She'd never put out on a nondate."

"Date, nondate." Ethan shrugged. "We're talking Nick Damone. Walking sex in jeans and oxfords. It's more like fate. A gimme."

"Thanks for the bad golf metaphor. And for thinking I'd throw myself at him, given the chance. I went there to talk, remember?"

"Don't get mad, Holls." He grinned at her over his burger. "We just need details."

"Yeah. What was the penthouse like?"

"Forget that. How did he kiss?"

Holly repressed the urge to smile. Sure, they were nosy. And frustrating as all get-out. But they meant well. "All you need to know is there's no way he'll work with me now."

"Actually…" Ethan and Noelle shared a nervous look and he went on, "Ted called this morning. Nick's on board. He's signing the contract as we speak."

"What?" Holly's fork clattered to the floor. The whole diner seemed to go quiet.

Noelle took her hand across the table. "We figured something must have happened between you two when you wouldn't return our phone calls. That's why I texted you to meet us here. We wanted to tell you ourselves. Together. In person."

"In public," Ethan added, scanning the crowded restaurant.

"You've got to stop this! I can't face him. Not after yesterday." Holly's cheeks burned at the memory of how she'd gyrated on Nick like a porn star. What had she been thinking? Oh, wait, that's right. She hadn't been thinking. Not with her brain, anyway.

"It's too late." Ethan was apologetic but firm. "The contract's a done deal. The investors are ecstatic."

"We're sorry, Holly." Noelle's voice was calm, reasonable and totally ineffective. "We never meant to hurt you. I swear."

"We screwed up," Ethan agreed. "Springing Nick on you. But we were only trying to help."

"This can't be happening." Holly pushed her still-full plate away, but it was too late. Her stomach lurched, making an awful sloshing noise that she swore could have been heard all the way to Hoboken. She was going to hurl. Right there.

"Look at it this way." Noelle poked at her own salad, sans chicken, cheese, nuts and dressing. Ballerinas! No wonder she was so darned skinny. "Whatever went on in that hotel room, it changed his mind about doing the show. And that was the point of your visit, right? So you done good."

"Noelle's right." Ethan stuffed a French fry into his mouth. "This is a good thing. For everyone."

Holly groaned and laid her head down on the table. "Not me."

"Yes, you." He nudged her under the table with his knee. "Didn't your therapist say you needed to get over your fear of intimacy? Since you and Nick got down and dirty…"

"We did not get down and dirty!" *Much.*

"…it would seem you've got that hurdle cleared."

"And there is no hurdle because I am not afraid of intimacy."

"Oh, sweetie." Noelle squeezed Holly's hand. "If you've got a hurdle, Nick's a great guy to jump."

"I hate you." Holly raised her head and shot them her best screw-you glower. "Both of you."

"Hate us all you want, Hollypop." Ethan flipped money onto the table for the check. "You're still stuck with Nick for the next eight weeks. At least."

Eight weeks. Eight long, excruciating weeks with the one man in the western hemisphere who could make her forget her name, address and Dramatists Guild number just by looking at her.

She was never going to make it.

Unless…

"Fine. But you have to promise me two things." Holly pointed a finger at Ethan's chest. "First, don't ever call me Hollypop in front of Nick Damone."

He nodded. "Done. What's the second thing?"

"Whatever you do, do not—under any circumstances— leave me alone with him."

NICK HAD TO find a way to get her alone.

He shifted in the painful metal folding chair. He should be focusing on the scene Malcolm and Marisa were rehearsing, or reviewing the script. Instead, he was fixated on Holly.

She was sitting only feet away across the tiny rehearsal room at Pearl Studios where they'd spent the majority of the past week, behind a table with Ethan and their stage manager, Jimmie Lee, looking more like the Holly he remembered from Stockton. She'd swapped the fancy clothes for cropped jeans and a flowery little top that did nothing to hide her cute little figure. The pink polish on her toes taunted him from the tips of her flip-flops. Her hair was brushed to one side like before but was softer now, her bangs falling gently across her forehead. And as far as he could tell, the only makeup she had on was that raspberry lip gloss he'd had so much fun kissing off.

But she might as well have been across the Grand Canyon for all the good it did him.

He continued to stare at her, trying to Jedi-mind-trick her into looking up from her script and acknowledging him. But just like every other damn day, she seemed intent on finding new ways to avoid him. Showing up at the last possible minute. Skipping out before lunch break. Running for the door the second they were done for the day.

How was he supposed to break down her defenses if she wouldn't even look at him? Maybe he could—

"Does that work for you, Nick?"

He snapped to attention at Ethan's voice. "Uh, sorry. I didn't catch that," he admitted, tapping his pencil on his script. "I was, um, making some notes on my character's backstory." *And plotting how to win over the playwright.*

"I'd like to run Malcolm and Marisa's scene one more time to fine-tune the blocking, then pick up from your entrance at the top of act two."

"Sure thing."

"I need a break," Malcolm huffed. "I'm dying of thirst. It's, like, a thousand degrees in here. What kind of low-rent production is this anyway? First the power goes out, then your caterer gives us food poisoning, now the air conditioning's on the fritz." He dropped onto a folding chair, took a sip from a bottle of water one of the production assistants handed him and grimaced. "And can I get some Evian, for Christ's sake? This cheap stuff tastes like crap."

"What about Thing One and Thing Two?" Nick asked, noticing for the first time that Malcolm's ever-present personal assistants, two recent Columbia film school grads eager for whatever showbiz scraps he threw their way, were missing. "Isn't that their job?"

"Sean's getting my dry cleaning. And Seth's waiting for the movers to deliver my big-screen TV."

Poor guys. Nick had left his assistant back home, to watch his house in Malibu and handle his fan mail. He wasn't such a diva that he couldn't go it alone for two months.

Unlike some people, he thought as Malcolm continued to gripe under his breath about the water.

"Take ten, everyone." Ethan pulled a bill out of his wallet and handed it to the production assistant. "Can you run down to the deli at the corner of Eighth and Thirty-seventh and get Mr. Justice his water?"

"Sure thing."

"Thanks, Wes." Holly rewarded the PA with a dazzling smile, reminding Nick of yet another reason he was so drawn to her. She knew everyone's name, even the interns. Refused to take the last bagel from the craft services table. Reacted to everything from a broken pipe to a dirty joke with a sense of humor and a quick laugh.

With a nod, Wes hurried out of the room, probably petrified "Mr. Justice," as Malcolm insisted the crew call him, would chew his head off if he didn't come back in under sixty seconds with a case of his precious Evian.

Self-centered, egotistical asshole.

But Nick didn't have time to dwell on Malcolm Justice and his parade of character flaws. He had ten minutes—well, more like nine now—to get to Holly before she disappeared on him again. If he was lucky, maybe he could get her to bestow one of those dazzling smiles on him.

He stuck his pencil in his script and stashed it under his chair, ready to make his move, when he felt a soft tap on his shoulder.

"Excuse me, Mr. Damone?" Marisa Rodriguez stood next to him, nervously biting her lip. With him and Malcolm on board, the producers had taken a chance on the young, relatively inexperienced actress for the pivotal role of the abused wife. From what he'd seen so far, their risk was going to pay off. She had a wonderful, natural quality that couldn't be taught in any acting class. "Can I ask you something?"

Nick snuck a glance at Holly and frowned. Ethan, her self-appointed bodyguard, had once again glued himself to her side. They sat together, shoulders touching, heads bowed over a copy of the script.

Jesus. The guy was like her freaking shadow. Nick wouldn't be surprised to find out they went to the damn bathroom together. At first he thought maybe they were a couple, with their constant chatter, light touches and little laughs. That illusion had been blessedly blown to bits when Ethan's boyfriend had shown up to meet him after rehearsal.

Still, Ethan needed to get accidentally locked in the prop room for a good half a day.

Overnight would be even better.

Nick turned back to his impressionable costar and flashed her a grin that he hoped was reassuring. "Of course." He patted the chair next to him, and Marisa sat down. "But I keep telling you, call me Nick. After all, we are married, in a manner of speaking."

She blushed and ducked her head, her mane of long dark curls covering her face. "Okay, Mr.... I mean, Nick."

"Now that we've got that settled, what can I do for you?"

"I'm just curious." She peered at him through her bangs. "You've done stage productions before, right?"

"It's been a while, but yeah."

"Are you nervous?"

"Not really," he lied. "It's like riding a bike. And nothing beats performing in front of a live audience. The instant response. The connection." *The chance that any minute you could forget your lines or your blocking. No one to bail you out by yelling, "Cut."*

"No, I mean because of the—" she stopped and looked around as if to make sure no one else was listening. When she spoke again, her voice was a whisper "—curse."

He rubbed the back of his neck. "The what?"

"The crew says we're cursed. Because of all the weird stuff going on. You know. The bomb threat. The food poisoning. The blackout."

Nick nodded, finally understanding. Of course Marisa would be worried. It was her plane that had been grounded by a bomb threat in Toronto, where she'd been wrapping a film, making her miss the first read-through. Then half the crew had gotten food poisoning from some bad sushi. And yesterday the power had gone out at Pearl, costing them half a day's practice.

But all shows hit rough waters, and Nick wasn't about to let Marisa drown in them. These were hiccups, not the *Titanic*.

"Nah," he assured her. "Theater people are suspicious by nature."

"Really?"

"Sure. That's why we say 'break a leg' instead of 'good luck.' And leave a ghost light on onstage. And, most importantly, never, ever say or quote from *Macbeth* in a theater."

Marisa tilted her head, looking confused. "What do you call it, then?"

"You don't." Nick chuckled. "Or, if you must, it's the Scottish play."

"That's silly."

"Yep. Like believing we're cursed is silly."

"I guess so. Thanks, Mr.... Nick. Sorry." She stood and stretched, showing a wide expanse of her flat stomach that, in another lifetime, one before Holly had reappeared, would have had him itching to see more. Now he wasn't interested. He ran a hand across his face, trying to erase the unfamiliar feeling.

"I think I'll get a Diet Coke from the vending machine in the hall." Marisa flipped her thick, dark curls over her shoulder. "Do you want anything?"

"No, thanks." He picked up a stainless-steel water bottle with the UCONN Huskies logo on it from the floor next to his chair. "Tap water's good enough for me."

"Score one for you," she said, her eyes flicking to Malcolm before she bounded off.

Nick leaned back in his chair, a trace of an amused smile playing around his lips. Smart girl. Perceptive, too. She was going to do just fine in this business.

He took a long, cool drink from the Huskies bottle and checked his watch. Ethan's ten minutes were almost up, and Wes and the Evian were still conspicuously absent. But instead of ranting and raving like the first-rate prima donna everyone knew he was, Malcolm was perched on the edge of the table next to Holly, with Ethan nowhere in sight.

Shit. The bastard had swooped in before Nick could react to the fact that she'd finally lost her guard dog. He'd been fawning all over her at every possible opportunity from the first day of rehearsal. Bringing her coffee in the morning. Complimenting her word choices in the script. Touching her whenever—wherever—he could.

Like now. Malcolm pulled a strand of her hair from his mouth and gave a low laugh.

Nick's fists clenched. If the guy got any closer his tongue would be in her eardrum. And at the rate it was drifting downward, the hand lazily caressing her back would be on her ass before long.

If Ethan was getting locked in a closet, Malcolm was

going into a Dumpster with a thick chain and padlock. And maybe a couple of hungry rats.

Nick sprang from his chair, slamming it into the wall behind him with a loud clang. *Fuck this.* He was done standing by while freaking Malcolm Justice made time with the woman who, barely more than a week ago, was melting into his kiss, panting at his touch, moaning his name.

Something had scared her off that day in his hotel room. One minute she'd been all over him, meeting his tongue thrust for thrust and grinding against him so hard he'd almost shot his load then and there. The next she was running for the door. He'd waited long enough to find out what had spooked her. Today he was getting some answers.

OH, CRAP.

Holly's stomach sank as she saw Nick stalking toward her, his forehead creased, the lips that had kissed her so wantonly pressed together.

"Excuse me, Malcolm," she said, interrupting another of his self-absorbed stories. This one, as far as she could tell, was building up to how he'd outsmarted Scorsese. "I'd better see if Ethan and the others have any questions."

"Justice." Nick cut in before she could break away. "You won't mind if I steal our illustrious author for a few minutes."

Malcolm reached for Holly's wrist but she shook him off. "As a matter of fact, I would."

"And why is that?"

"I don't think that's any of your business, Damone."

"I'm making it my business."

"Not if I can help it."

"Stop, both of you!" Holly's head ached from pinging back and forth between them. "You're acting like a couple of overgrown frat boys, arguing over me as if I weren't standing right in front of you."

They continued to glare at each other over her head for a moment, making her feel a little like a choice sirloin in the middle of two hungry dogs. Was it possible to be flattered and disgusted at the same time?

Nick was the one to finally concede the staring contest. "Holly." He put a hand on her elbow, his touch not demanding but imploring, those beautiful brown eyes sucking her in closer. Heat spread from his fingers to her traitorous girlie bits. "I just need a few minutes of your time. To... discuss my role."

"Don't you mean 'show you my etchings'?" Malcolm leered.

Nick's attention didn't waver from Holly. "Please."

If he had begged, pleaded, ranted, raved—anything but that one simple, quiet word—she could have fought him.

Two more weeks. That's all she needed. Then they'd be in the Deville, the theater they'd call home for the foreseeable future. She'd be able to keep her distance from him in that cavern, her in the house with the rest of the creative team and him up onstage or in the wings.

But no. He'd managed to corner her today in the cramped rehearsal room, all intense and brooding and yeah, mouthwateringly hot in a Mr. Darcy kind of way, with those puppy-dog eyes and his hair flopping over his brows, a tad long and just this side of presentable.

"You don't have to go with him, Holly." Malcolm went for her wrist again but she managed to sidestep him. Ugh. He was a good actor, she'd give him that. Good-looking, too, although he didn't make her stammer like a fool or bump into the furniture. That was apparently reserved for Nick.

But as talented and handsome as he was, Malcolm

couldn't take a hint to save his life. She'd told him flat-out that she wasn't interested in him. But he still insisted on hounding her, at her side practically every time she turned around. The only plus was it had kept Nick at bay. Until now.

"It's okay." As if she really had a choice. Better to get it over with, painful but quick. "We won't be long."

"You're going to let this guy—"

"I'm not going to 'let' him do anything." She gave a meaningful look to both men. After Clark—and a fair amount of therapy—she'd made up her mind not to let any man have that kind of power over her ever again. And these two were no exception. She was the one calling the shots now. "But I am going to talk to him."

Nick's hand on her elbow gently navigated her to the door as he called over his shoulder to Malcolm, "Tell Ethan we'll be down the hall, in studio G. If we're not back in time, start without us."

"I'm not your errand boy, Damone."

"Then have Sean or Seth do it. It's a step above the crap you usually palm off on them." Nick continued down the hall, pulling Holly along with him. He didn't speak again until they were inside the room with the door closed.

"Start talking."

She arched a brow at him. "What?"

"You told Justice you were going to talk to me. So talk."

"About your role?"

"You know damn well that's not why I brought you here."

"I'm not a mind reader." She shook his hand off her elbow and stepped away from him, making her raging hor-mones scream in protest. Not to mention her conscience. Giving Nick the cold shoulder went against every rule of politeness and common decency she'd had drummed into her since childhood. But it was a matter of self-preservation, pure and simple. "If this isn't about the show, we have nothing to discuss."

"Like hell we don't." He crossed his arms, looking yummy with his long denim-clad legs braced apart, his biceps straining at his shirt sleeves.

"What do you want from me, Nick?"

"I want to know what kind of game you're playing."

"Game?"

"First me. Now Justice." Nick's eyes were narrowed, his lips tight.

Holly gaped at him. He was jealous! Nick Damone was actually jealous. Over her. She covered her mouth and let out a giggle.

"What's so funny?"

"Just wondering about the pigs."

"Pigs?" The tension around his eyes relaxed and his mouth curved into the tiniest hint of a smile.

The ones that must be flying over the Manhattan skyline. "Never mind." She scraped her hands through her hair. He made her crazy. "Look, nothing's going on between me and Malcolm. Or me and you, for that matter."

"You sure about that?" His wicked chocolate eyes, almost black with need, lasciviously perused her from head to toe and back again.

"Yes," she choked out through a heavy swallow, her heart racing.

"You can't run forever, Holly."

She sighed, knowing he was right. "I can sure as heck try."

"You're going to have to try a lot harder to shake me, sweetheart." He pushed off the doorframe, chest muscles rippling under his tight T-shirt—darn it if her own chest didn't rise to attention—and started toward her.

She took two steps back—straight into a table.

"See?" He inched one leg between hers and braced a hand on the tabletop. "No more running."

"It certainly seems that way." She took a deep breath meant to steady her. Instead it brought her closer to him, brushing her already aching nipples against his rock-hard pecs and making her shiver.

"So you're ready to admit defeat?"

She raised herself up on tiptoe, her lips only inches from his. "I—"

The door flung open to reveal Wes, back from his errand, red-faced and wheezing.

"Nick, Holly! Come quick! You're not gonna believe this!"

"What is it?" Holly silently thanked the powers that be for the interruption.

"The Deville's on fire!"

6

HOLLY STARED, GLASSY-EYED and numb, at the TV screen above the bar, showing the smoldering Deville for the umpteenth time. How could she be dead-tired and wide-awake at the same time?

The fire was out but the damage was done. They'd never find another theater before losing their cast.

Two years of planning. Up in smoke.

She tapped her glass on the gleaming oak bar. "Can I get a refill, Devin?"

"You sure?" The bartender grabbed the remote from under the counter and switched the channel to one of the sports networks. Baseball. Much better, even if the Yankees were getting spanked by the Blue Jays. "It's a lot stronger than your usual."

"I'm sure." After today, she needed something way more potent than a mudslide.

"Okay." Devin grabbed a bottle from the shelf behind her and poured two fingers of rich amber liquid into Holly's glass. "But after this I'm switching you to Kahlúa and milk."

"Killjoy." Holly took a sip and coughed. Why anyone drank Scotch was beyond her. But tonight she wanted—no, needed—to get drunk, so Scotch it was.

"Looks to me like there's not much joy to kill."

Holly sighed. Her friend was right. Tonight there was no joy in Mudville. Flighty Holly had struck out.

Watching the Deville burn on the news had been surreal. The cast and crew had all huddled around Ethan's laptop, silent. A few of them had wanted to head over to the theater, but Ted and Judith—when they weren't sniping at each other—convinced them they'd only get in the way. After about a dozen replays, they'd sent almost everyone home with the promise of an email by morning. Only Holly, Ethan and the company manager had stayed, frantically calling every theater in a twenty-block radius.

The Helen Hayes was too small. The Gershwin too big. The Lyceum was just right but unavailable. As were the Cort, the Booth and the Walter Kerr. Four hours of speed dialing and all they had to show for it were sore fingers and an air of desperation.

"Go home, Holly," Ethan had ordered when she laid her head on the table and let gravity and fatigue keep it there. "We've got things covered here. I'll call you if anything pans out."

She pushed herself upright on leaden arms. There had to be something more she could do. Make a latte run. Recharge phones. Pay a visit to someone and beg.

Oh, wait. She'd already done that with Nick, and look where that had gotten her.

Ethan had won out in the end. Sort of. She'd gone, but not home. Instead, she'd stopped by Naboombu, the cozy underground bar around the corner from her East Village apartment, where Devin Padilla, her upstairs neighbor and best NYC gal pal, tended bar. If Holly was going to drown her sorrows, she could count on Devin to drag her home.

They made an odd pair. Holly, the suburban-housewife refugee. Devin, with her multiple piercings and tattoos. But Devin's recent bad breakup had required just as much ice cream as Holly's divorce, and they'd commiserated over multiple pints of Ben & Jerry's Karamel Sutra.

"So what happens now?" Devin picked up a cloth and swirled circles down the length of the bar.

Holly knocked down another swig of Scotch. "Beats me."

She checked her cell phone for what must have been the hundredth time. No messages. Four bars. And yes, the ringer was on high. "But if this show goes belly-up before it even opens, it'll take years for me to get another shot at Broadway."

"Why? It's not your fault the place burned down."

"That's not the point. The fire's just the latest—and worst—in a string of catastrophes. It's like the show's doomed. No one's going to want to take a chance on it. Or on me."

A man at the opposite end of the bar raised his empty mug and eyeballed Devin. With a sympathetic look at Holly, she tossed the cloth onto her shoulder and went to refill the guy's beer, leaving Holly alone with her Scotch and fatalistic attitude. A dangerous combination, if there ever was one. What if they couldn't find another theater? What if the show had to be canceled? What if Nick left town and they never got a chance to finish what they'd started in his hotel room?

Stop. Wait. Whoa. Where the heck had that come from? Holly downed the rest of her Scotch, hoping the burning sensation would erase her last thought. It didn't.

She so did not want to go there, but once her brain started down that dangerous path, her thoughts filled with images of her and Nick. Naked, sweaty and entwined.

It was official. She was an idiot. She'd had the man of her dreams in the palm of her hand—literally, she thought, remembering the feel of his smooth, bare chest—

and she'd blown it. What was she so worried about? Her scars? Badges of honor. She was a survivor of domestic violence and should be proud of it, not hiding like a scared rabbit. The fact that she and Nick were working together? Big deal. Coworkers hooked up all the time. Wasn't Noelle always going on about the affaires de coeur in the corps de ballet?

And that point would be moot soon anyway. Without a theater, there wouldn't be a show. And without a show, she'd be collecting unemployment. Or walking dogs again, her family whispering behind her back about the demise of yet another one of "Holly's follies." Nick would go back to playing superheroes for billions. Or maybe he'd branch out into ancient warriors or Greek gods.

"You think too much." Devin was back, replacing Holly's empty glass with a tumbler of foamy white liquid. "I'm afraid to ask what's going on in there sometimes."

"Don't." Holly sipped the frothy concoction, hoping the rich, sweet taste would obliterate the lingering flavor of the Scotch and the memory of Nick's kiss.

"Whatever it is, I'm jealous." Devin strong-armed a tray of glasses onto the bar and grabbed a clean towel to wipe them dry. "I could swear there's steam rising off your skin."

"It's steamy, all right."

"Then it must involve your Hottie McHothot movie star."

"He is not *my* movie star." Holly shook her head, regretting her decision in a moment of girl-bonding over a *True Blood* marathon to tell Devin about her renewed obsession with Nick.

"But he could be."

"What makes you say that?"

Devin smiled and waved her towel at the door. "He just walked in."

"Not funny." But normally cool, biker-tough Devin was beaming like an awestruck fangirl. Holly's stomach dropped.

"No way," she whispered.

"Way," Devin mouthed back.

Holly spun on her stool, and there was Nick walking toward her, nine kinds of fine in a black leather jacket, heather-gray T-shirt and his customary jeans, faded and seemingly shrink-wrapped to his thighs. In a few strides, he crossed the narrow bar and was at her side.

"Okay if I sit here?"

Those five words took her back fifteen years. She eyed Nick, wondering if he realized he'd said the same thing to her on the dock that night?

"Feel free," she answered, trying to sound indifferent. Not an easy feat when just the sound of his voice made her whole body hum like a tuning fork. At least this time she'd managed more than "Uh, yeah."

And then he was next to her. Sitting. Leaning. His knee brushed hers, ratcheting the hum up to a dull roar.

Devin ditched the towel and leaned against the bar, giving Nick an eyeful of her ample cleavage. "What can I get you?"

"Traitor," Holly muttered, shooting daggers at her. Devin smiled and shrugged as if to say, *You're not interested. That makes him fair game. Right?*

Right, Holly told herself. *Not interested. Fair game.* No matter what her mutinous, pulsating body said.

"Scotch." Nick placed his order, either completely oblivious to her back-and-forth with Devin or totally ignoring it. "Neat. Macallan, if you have it."

"We might. For you." Devin swept a hand through her

long dark hair and Holly fought the urge to leap over the bar and tackle her. "Let me check the boss's private stock."

"How come he gets the good stuff?" Holly complained.

Nick shifted in his seat and his leg brushed hers again, shooting her pulse into the red zone. "Maybe because I can tell the difference."

"There's that," Devin cooed, batting her thick, full eyelashes at him. The hussy. "Plus, you're prettier than her. And you asked real polite. Besides," she continued, turning to Holly, "I've been watering yours down when you weren't looking. Otherwise you'd be on the floor by now. No bartender worth her salt would do that to Macallan."

"Amen to that." Nick raised a mock glass in salute.

"Thanks a lot," Holly grumbled. No wonder she didn't feel wasted.

"You kids play nice until I get back," Devin called over her shoulder as she sashayed around the bar. "And if Frankie down there at the end wants another, tell him he's cut off."

"As if," Holly fired back but not quickly enough. Devin disappeared down the hall leading to the office and storage room.

"Friend of yours?" Nick asked.

"Yeah. You can autograph her chest later." Holly toyed with the swizzle stick in her drink. "How did you find me?"

"Ethan. He gave me your address. Said if you weren't there, you'd probably be here."

Wow. He'd wormed her address out of Ethan—which, okay, probably wasn't that hard—trekked all the way downtown, then followed her to Naboombu. All so he could... What? Hold her hand? Dry her tears? Or maybe he planned to console her more...intimately.

Holly's breath quickened at the thought and she pressed

her cold glass against her cheek in a vain attempt to stop the flush she felt from spreading across her face. Did Nick still want her? Was that why he'd tracked her down? And what if he did?

"I spoke with Ted."

Nick's voice was like a bucket of cold water doused over her head. Of course, he was here to discuss the show. "Any progress?" she asked hopefully.

He shook his head. "It doesn't look good. Everything suitable is booked until fall. Which wouldn't be so bad, except…"

"Except if we wait that long we risk losing you."

"Unfortunately."

"And Malcolm."

"Now, *that* would be tragic," he drawled.

Devin came back with Nick's Scotch and they drank silently while she went to handle Frankie, who was banging his mug impatiently on the bar.

Nick was the one to break the silence. "I'm sorry, Holly," he said. "I wish…"

"I know." After a long pause, she asked, "Will you go back to L.A.?"

"Dunno. Probably." He leaned back, swirling the Scotch around in his glass. "Maybe make a quick stop home first."

"Stockton?"

He nodded and stared into his drink.

"When was the last time you were there?"

"Fifteen years ago."

"You mean you haven't been back?"

"Nope." He lifted his glass and downed the contents. "Not since I left."

"What about your parents?" As much as they sometimes annoyed her, Holly couldn't imagine going that long without seeing her family. Even during the last few years of her marriage, when Clark had done his best to cut her off from the rest of the world, she'd managed to see them on holidays.

"My mom visits me on the West Coast twice a year."

"And your dad?"

A hint of the vulnerable teenager she'd seen that night at the cast party flashed across Nick's handsome face. "He doesn't travel."

"Oh." She watched his expression flatten and calm, the boy within him disappearing. Nick was a man toughened—and blessed—by life. But maybe he was as much of a screw-up in his family as anyone else.

As much as her.

He tunneled a hand through his luscious, too-long locks and dropped his empty glass down on the bar. "Enough about me. I came here to make sure you're okay. Unless you'd rather be alone…"

"I'm…" She started to give her standard "I'm fine," then stopped. She wasn't fine. She was a churning mass of competing emotions, not one of them "fine." And the last thing she wanted was to be alone.

What she wanted was Nick. Touching her. Kissing her. Making her forget that the show she'd banked her reputation on was dead in the water, that she'd soon be back in Stockton, living with her parents. And while she didn't want to go fifteen years without seeing them, moving in with them wasn't exactly part of her master plan.

Holly knew if she and Nick picked up where they'd left off that day in his hotel room, they weren't going to stop with touching and kissing. She also knew he'd be gone before she could say off-off-Broadway, back to the sun, surf and starlets in L.A. But she didn't care. Nick was here with her now.

And it wasn't as if she was looking for anything permanent. She'd been there, done that, gone down in flames. Clark had seemed so harmless, the prototypical mild-mannered science geek, complete with glasses and pocket protector. Yet marrying him had wound up being the most dangerous decision she'd ever made.

Sleeping with Nick would be dangerous, too, but for far different reasons. He might not pose a threat to her body—at least not the way Clark had—but there was a good chance that, if she let him, he could walk away with her heart and soul. A real triple threat, never mind the whole acting, singing and dancing thing.

So just make sure you don't let him, she told herself. Easier said than done, but the heat coursing through her body—whether from the alcohol or Nick's earthy, totally male scent—was telling her it was time she started taking some risks in her personal life. And Nick Damone was six foot plus of heart-stopping, lip-smacking risk personified.

"I'm glad you're here. I could use some company tonight."

"At your service." He gestured toward her half-empty glass. "Can I buy you another?"

"Actually, I was thinking we should…"

"Should?" He inched his bar stool closer to hers.

"Maybe…"

"Maybe?"

She stared up at the ball game on TV. If she looked at him, she'd never get out what she needed to say. As it was, her words came out in a breathless rush. "Go somewhere a little more private."

She felt Nick tense beside her. Heard him inhale sharply. "Where did you have in mind?"

He rested his arm on the back of her bar stool, skimming her shoulder with his fingers. Heat radiated down her arm and crackled across her chest. She couldn't breathe, couldn't believe she was going to do this. She took a hefty slug of her mudslide for Dutch courage and turned to him, running a hand up his leg until it came to rest on his thigh, dangerously close to his crotch so he couldn't possibly misunderstand her. His muscles twitched under her palm.

"My place."

7

He was the luckiest son of a bitch on earth.

"Are you sure?" Nick asked.

Holly nodded. "Positive." Her voice, low and breathy, crawled up his spine like naughty fingers, leaving a trail of goose bumps in their wake. "One night before you go. No strings."

He threw a stack of bills down on the bar, not bothering to count them, and grabbed the hand that was only millimeters from his throbbing dick. "Then let's get out of here," he growled, pulling her up from the stool and practically dragging her toward the door. He pushed it open, blasting them with warm air.

"Leaving so soon?" Devin hollered after them.

"I'll text you," Holly called back.

"Tomorrow," Nick added as he hauled her outside, the door slamming shut behind them. He looked left, then right, relieved to find the street virtually deserted. Not a paparazzo in sight. The New York photogs were way less vigilant than their L.A. counterparts. Yet another check in the pros column for the Big Apple. Just to be safe, he hung a sharp right and rounded the corner of the bar, moving them away from the glare of the streetlights and into a dark, shadowy alley along the side of the building.

"My apartment's that way," Holly protested, pointing in the opposite direction.

"First this." He backed her against the wall and planted a palm on either side of her head, against the rough brick. With one knee, he nudged her legs apart and edged between them. Dipping his head, he captured her lips, first gently, coaxing them open with a sweep of his tongue, then, when he felt her arch against his chest, more deeply, more forcefully.

He lowered his hands and cupped her sweet, round ass. He squeezed lightly, savoring the feel of her, all soft and warm. Like a woman should feel. A far cry from the stick figures in Hollywood.

He tugged her closer for a better fit, molding her to him so she could feel his rock-hard erection. She gasped and he pulled back, raising his head to look at her. Her eyes shone and her breathing was choppy. He couldn't tell if she wanted to hit him or jump his bones.

Nick fought for control of his own ragged breathing. "Maybe we should…"

Holly surprised him by grabbing the collar of his jacket and dragging him back to her. "Too much talking. Not enough kissing." She slid her arms around his neck and tangled her fingers in the hair at his nape, pressing her hot body against his and pulling his head down even farther so her lips could reach his. She kissed him wildly, thrusting her tongue against his and tilting her hips to bring her warm, wet center in contact with the zipper straining to hold back his cock.

Groaning, he broke off this kiss, thinking it would slow her down so he could prolong both their pleasure. But slowing down didn't seem to be part of her game plan. Instead, she let her mouth drift to his neck, leaving a trail of kisses and tender bites from his chin to the base of his throat.

"Damn, I want you," he growled.

"So I see," she teased, rubbing against the bulge in his jeans. "Do you plan to do anything about it?"

"Hell, yes."

He lifted her up, cupping her bottom. Still pressed against the brick wall, she wrapped her legs around him and ran her fingers through his hair.

"Nick…" She sighed, grinding against him. "More."

She didn't have to ask twice. Following her lead, he tasted her soft earlobe then moved his mouth slowly down her neck, nibbling lightly. With one hand he released the top button of her blouse, then another, revealing just a hint of her lacy baby-blue bra. His lips followed, the stubble of his beard scraping the sensitive skin between her breasts and making her moan.

It was crazy, what they were doing. Outside, in public, at barely eleven o'clock. When anyone could come along. He was long past caring, though, and, thankfully, so was she.

He freed one more button, running the tip of his tongue deep into her cleavage. She whimpered as he undid the front clasp of her bra with his teeth, releasing her pale breasts, two perfect handfuls topped by pert, rosy nipples begging to be sucked. He looked up at her, her head thrown back, eyes wide, hair mussed. Her mouth was open, her lips full and moist. She'd been transformed into a wild, wanton goddess, and he had to have her. Now.

He drew one nipple into his mouth, rolling the taut bud with his tongue. She tasted like cinnamon and sugar and warm, soft woman. He dragged his mouth across her chest to savor the other nipple. A strange humming sensation built inside him as he sucked and licked like a starving man at an all-you-can-eat buffet.

"Nick."

"Mmm." The humming intensified, spreading throughout his chest.

"Your phone."

He reluctantly let go of her breast and lifted his head. "Huh?"

"Your phone. It's buzzing."

He set her down and reached into his jacket pocket, pulling out his cell. A message flashed that he had one new text. Without even bothering to read it, he turned the phone off and put it back in his pocket.

"Aren't you going to…"

"No."

"But what if it's Ethan or Ted or Judith…" With trembling fingers, she struggled to fasten her bra. "Maybe this was a bad idea."

She was freaking out. That was okay. He'd been about to take her against a brick wall. He wrapped her delicate hands in his own, the heat between them making him sweat. "You said you wanted one night, right?"

"I think we both know why it can't be anything more than that."

Yeah, he knew. His career on the other coast. The fame. His shitty childhood and resulting commitment phobia. It all made him a terrible candidate for a long-term relationship. So why was he so reluctant to agree with her?

"Then you've got it," he said after a long moment, swallowing his doubts. He moved her hands aside and fastened first her bra then the buttons on her blouse. "One night. You and me. No interruptions."

He'd barely finished speaking when something chimed in her messenger bag, which had fallen to the ground at her feet during their free-for-all. Wordlessly, she picked it up and retrieved her cell phone.

"No interruptions," she echoed, meeting his gaze.

With a flourish, she held down the end-call button and dropped the phone back into her bag.

"I'LL GET US a cab." Nick strode toward the street, leaving Holly to finish putting herself back together.

As if on cue, a cab turned the corner, its top light on to show that it was available. The man really did lead a charmed life. Putting two fingers in his mouth, he let loose a shrill whistle, and the cab pulled to the curb. "If I've only got one night with you, I'm going to make it count."

Only one night? What was he trying to say? Did he want more than one night? With her?

Oh, she knew he wanted her. She'd felt the proof of that in the alley. But for more than one night? No way. He'd be history once they'd scratched the irresistible itch that was pulling them together. He'd admitted as much earlier when he told her he'd be heading back to L.A. now that the play was no go.

But that didn't mean she was going to give up her chance at a night of mad passion under Nick's skilled hands—hands that could wipe away some of the sting of the wounds Clark had left, inside and out.

"Trust me?"

She hesitated, knowing this was her last chance to back out. She hitched her bag up on her shoulder and put her hand in his. "Let's go."

He opened the rear door and helped her inside. "Plaza Hotel."

She eyed him, brows raised. "We're putting you up at the Plaza?"

"No," he said, laughing softly. "I bought one of the condo suites a few months ago. I had some renovations done, and it wasn't ready for me to move in until last week."

He dropped an arm over her shoulders and scooted her

closer to him. "You'll be my first guest." His breath was warm and smelled of whiskey, stirring the hair around her ear. "It's got a king-size bed. A whirlpool bath that fits two. I think I've even got a pint of Ben & Jerry's in the freezer."

"What girl could say no to Ben and Jerry?"

"And here I thought it was me you couldn't say no to." He squeezed between her neck and shoulder and she melted, unable to move. With one finger he pushed aside the collar of her blouse and bent his head to kiss the newly exposed skin. He licked the same spot, trailing his tongue up her neck to her ear. "Can you, Holly? Say no to me?"

Her head fell back and she swayed into him. "Um," she said dazedly. There were no words.

He peppered hot, wet kisses along her jawline. "Now, *that's* what I like to hear."

"Nick," she hissed when his lips traveled down her neck toward the valley between her breasts. "The cabbie."

"Don't worry, sweetheart. It's New York. He's seen it all." His free hand moved to the inside of her thigh and pushed her legs apart. "Besides, he's not paying any attention to us."

"I... Oh." A moan escaped her parted lips when his wayward hand journeyed higher to stroke her through her sopping-wet jeans.

"Shh," he warned, bringing his mouth to hers. "You don't want him to hear you, do you?"

"No, but..." He ground the heel of his hand against her and she moaned louder.

"You leave me no choice," he murmured against her lips. "Got to keep you quiet somehow."

He planted his mouth on hers, instantly hot and demanding. She arched her back and ran a hand up his chest, clutching the fabric of his T-shirt as if it were an anchor that could stop her from drifting away on a wave of sheer sensuality.

They stayed locked together until he raised his head, making her whimper in protest. "It's okay, babe. We're here."

The cab slowed to a stop and Holly looked up to see the famous façade of the Plaza.

"That'll be twenty bucks, Mr. Damone." The cabbie turned and gave a little cough. "And, uh, can I have your autograph? For my wife. She's a big fan."

"Sure." Nick scrawled his signature on a napkin the cabbie gave him, handing it back along with the fare and what looked to be a sizable tip. Then he grabbed Holly's messenger bag and helped her out. She hummed with happy anticipation, her stomach quivering with sudden nerves as they crossed the palatial lobby. She barely registered the smiling doorman, the gold-leaf ceiling, the marble floor, on their way to the elevator.

"Come here." Nick reached for her again the second the doors slid shut. She went willingly into his arms, tilting her chin up and offering her lips. He accepted, lifting her up and devouring her mouth in a hot, hungry kiss.

Ding.

"Saved by the bell." The elevator jerked to a stop and Nick relaxed his hold, letting her slide down his body. She felt every ridge and curve of him, making her already pounding heart race even faster. With one arm wrapped possessively around her waist, he led her out of the elevator and down the hall to his door. He fumbled with the key and she smiled, relieved she wasn't the only one on edge. Finally, the door swung open and he ushered her inside, tossing off his jacket and flipping on lights as they went.

The place was like something out of a fairy tale, with plush carpeting, a marble fireplace and intricately carved furniture, all done in discreet, muted tones. Framed photographs of sunrises and sunsets added splashes of color. Through an open doorway she could see half of what appeared to be an enormous bed, topped by an elaborate headboard and covered by a brilliantly white duvet and matching pillows.

"Ice cream's in the butler's pantry." Nick came up behind her, one hand caressing her backside and his mouth on her neck. His lips were warm and wet against her skin. With his other hand he reached around to cup her breast. "If you're still hungry."

"I'm hungry," she said, leaning back into him. She could feel his erection, hot and hard, nestled in the space between her buttocks. "But not for Ben. Or Jerry."

In one fluid movement, he turned her in his arms and picked her up, cradling her to his chest. With long, purposeful strides, he carried her to the bedroom. If she thought she was in a fantasy before, now she was convinced. It was every sex dream she'd ever sweated through and twisted awake from with disappointment. Except she wasn't dreaming now, and she wasn't disappointed.

He paused just inside the door and groped for the light switch. Holly grabbed his wrist, stopping him. "No, please," she whispered. In the dark he wouldn't see the scars left by Clark's belt. She could tell herself all she wanted they were just something she'd gone through, scars from an emotional car wreck, but she wasn't ready to go there yet. Letting herself touch and be touched was a big enough step for now. "It's been a while since I've…been with anyone. I'd feel more comfortable if we left the lights off."

"How about a compromise." He slid the dimmer switch up a notch, bathing the room in a soft, blue-gray light. "As for the rest…" He moved his hand up to her cheek and brushed a stray lock of hair behind her ear. She could almost hear the smile in his voice. "I guess we'll just have to feel our way through."

She shook at the thought of feeling her way across his toned torso, down the hills and valleys of his abs and into the hollows where his hips met his pelvis. "That sounds... nice."

"*Nice* doesn't even begin to describe what we're going to do to each other, sweetheart." He crossed the room to the bed, letting her slide to her feet along his solid, muscular frame. One arm snaked around her back and molded her to him. The other hand still cradled her cheek, forcing her to look at him as he spoke, his voice husky. "I plan to explore every inch of your gorgeous body, from those perfect, pouty lips to the tips of your pretty little toes. I'm going to touch and kiss and nibble and lick you all over until you're begging me to let you come. And then, I'm going to start all over again."

Oh. My. God. Her body thrummed with sexual energy. No one had ever talked to her like this, so erotic. No one had ever wanted her like this, so openly. She felt like ice cream in a hot-fudge sundae, melting and dripping under the warm chocolate.

"And because I'm a fair-minded kind of guy," he continued, his lips moving closer to hers, "my body's yours for the taking, too. Nibble and lick wherever you like. As much as you like."

She sagged against him, every nerve ending screaming to be touched next.

"You okay?"

Voiceless, she could only nod.

"Good." His lips edged closer. "Because I'm going to explode if I have to wait one more minute to do this."

The hand on her cheek slid to cradle the back of her

neck, holding her captive as his lips met hers in a kiss that stole her breath. His tongue darted out to stroke hers and she moaned into his mouth, relishing the taste and feel of him. Pulling away slightly, he gently sucked first her upper lip, then her lower one, giving each a little nip before releasing it. Then it was her turn to nibble at his mouth, her tongue skating across his lips until they were both flushed and panting.

"Time for bed," he said with a growl, backing her into the mattress.

She fell with a squeal onto the soft duvet, loving the way it enveloped her. He stretched out beside her, their bodies touching from hip to toe, his head propped up by one hand. The other lingered over the waistband of her jeans.

"Tell me what you want."

His words, hoarse and quietly demanding, had her insides doing somersaults and her brain working overtime. What *did* she want? She'd never really thought about that before. Her admittedly limited sexual experience had been mostly about the guy getting off, not her own pleasure. It had certainly been that way with Clark. And the only orgasms she'd had in recent memory were self-induced.

"Talk to me, Holly." The hand over her waistband traveled across her body, gently kneading her hip. "I want to make you feel good."

"I…I do feel good," she gasped.

"Then I want to make you feel even better." He wedged one leg in between hers and she couldn't help but clamp her own legs around him.

Sighing, she rubbed against his tight, muscular thigh. "I'm not sure that's possible."

"It's possible." He freed the top two buttons of her blouse and pulled it off her shoulders. Her bra straps followed, pinning her upper arms to her body. "Let me show you." With one finger he ran a languorous trail from her chin down her neck to the valley between her breasts.

"I believe you," she whimpered, arching into him. "You're very convincing."

"I try." He chuckled, pulling down one bra cup to expose her nipple. "Points for effort." He shifted on the bed and bent to trace the curve of her breast with his tongue, making her swear it was lava, the way his touch burned her skin.

The other side of her bra got the same treatment, allowing his mouth to roam from one breast to the other. He took his sweet time teasing her, kissing and licking in circles but ignoring her aching nipples. When he lifted his head and gave her a wicked grin, she knew his omission was not accident.

"Please, Nick."

"Please what?" He nuzzled her chest, his tongue stealing out to lick the inside of each breast. "You can tell me. Don't be afraid."

Strangely, she wasn't. She trusted Nick to take care of her, felt safe with him even as he drove her wild with desire. She wanted to answer him, to let him know what she wanted. Besides, her stiff, swollen nipples couldn't take much more delicious torment. "Touch me," she begged. "Please."

"I am touching you." He brushed his fingertips over her stomach and up her rib cage, stopping just under the swell of her breasts where her shirt and bra were gathered. The bastard.

"Here," she choked out, cupping one breast and pinching the hard tip between her thumb and forefinger. "I need you to touch me here."

"Mmm." He placed a hand over hers and squeezed,

bringing the throbbing peak near his mouth. His hot breath blew across it when he spoke. "So pretty. Plump and pink."

"Nick…"

"And sensitive." Another gust of warm air wafted across her nipple and she practically came right there.

"I can't take much more," she cried out, biting her lip.

"Would you like my hands on you?" With one finger he grazed the edge of her tightly puckered areola, then withdrew. "Teasing those perfect buds until you fall apart in my arms? Or maybe…"

"Yes," she gasped when—*finally*—he followed his breath with his mouth, closing his lips around the rigid tip and sucking greedily. His hand moved to her other breast, finding and flicking the rosy crest with his thumb.

He lingered there, bringing her to the brink of ecstasy again and again before pulling back, denying her release. She moaned and clutched at his head, threading her fingers through his thick, dark hair in a desperate attempt to pump up the action. Her hips rocked against him as she tried to take herself over the edge he seemed so determined to keep out of reach.

Just when she thought she was as frustrated as she could get, he abandoned her breasts, kissing and caressing his way down her body to the waistband of her jeans. With one hand, he deftly released the snap and lowered the zipper inch by inch, his fingers barely skimming the pale blue silk of panties that matched her bra. She closed her eyes as he slipped one finger under the elastic to find her warm, wet crease.

"Holly."

His eyes were heavy-lidded and so dark they looked almost black.

"I want you to watch me. And I want to see those pretty green eyes when you come for me for the first time."

The first time? She licked her lips, her lust-addled brain struggling to process the images his words had planted there. Nick making her come with his fingers. Then his tongue. Then…

"Ah!" Holly inhaled sharply as he slid a finger inside her, stroking her deeply and making the fire that had been building in her belly rage out of control. Her sex pulsed against him and she arched up off the bed, needing to press even closer to the man who had pushed past her fears and awakened her slumbering sex drive.

"So wet," he murmured, adding a finger and thrusting deeper into her. "For me."

Too soon, he removed his fingers, but she forgave him when he replaced them with his mouth, blowing soft and warm on the silk of her panties. His hands went to her hips, lifting them up and slowly pulling her jeans and underwear down her legs to her ankles. She helped him by kicking off her ballet flats so he could remove them completely, leaving her prone, half-naked and vulnerable before him.

And just like that, her insecurities reared up. Nick had been great so far, a thoughtful and generous lover. But Clark had been great, too, at first. A lump formed in the pit of her stomach. Although she and Nick had known each other for years, she didn't really know him at all.

She grabbed one of the pillows and held it in front of her, shielding herself from those sinful chocolate eyes that were raking her up and down, making her flesh tingle from head to toe. "Nick, I…"

"What's wrong, babe?" In an instant, his eyes changed from wicked to worried, making her heart twist. She almost chucked the pillow on the floor and threw herself at him. Almost. But her old fears stood in her way like an impenetrable wall.

"I just…I can't—"

"It's okay," he cut in softly, sitting up beside her and giving her a little much-appreciated breathing room. "I'll stop if you want me to. I won't pretend I'm not disappointed, but I'll stop. Just give me the word."

She'd give him the word, all right. Goodbye. Adios. Sayonara. That was what her head was telling her to say. But apparently her wayward heart had gained control of her mouth, because when she opened it the word that came out was "Snicklefritz."

"Snicklefritz?" he repeated, the corners of his mouth curling into a grin.

"My therapist suggested I pick a safe word," she explained. "It's from a book I read as a kid."

If he wondered why she needed a therapist—or a safe word—he didn't let on. Instead, he merely nodded and said, "Snicklefritz it is, then."

"So, if I say it, we'll stop?" she asked, a seed of trust beginning to sprout deep inside her.

"I swear." He held up three fingers as if taking the Boy Scout oath.

With those two little words, her anxiety evaporated as quickly as it had appeared. "I seriously doubt you were ever a Boy Scout," she said, relaxing her death grip on the pillow and allowing herself to smile.

"No, I wasn't," he admitted, deadly serious now, his eyes intent and his mouth firm. "But I am a man of honor. And as much as I want to take you every which way imaginable, I promise to stop the minute you say so."

A man of honor. Ultimately, that was what separated Nick from Clark. There wasn't an honorable bone in Clark's miserable body. But somehow she knew Nick would keep his word.

Slowly, she released the pillow and let it fall to the side, baring herself once again for his appraisal. "Thank you," she whispered, the heat within her reigniting as his eyes swept over her. How could this man affect her so swiftly and so strongly? She felt like a kind of human sports car capable of going from zero to ready-and-willing in no time flat.

"No, sweetheart," Nick countered, lowering himself over her and planting a soft kiss on her hip. "Thank *you.*"

His hands moved to her inner thighs, gently pushing them apart. She knew what was coming next but still wasn't prepared for the delicious sensation of his mouth closing around her, the stubble of his beard scraping over her damp curls. With each swipe of his tongue he brought her closer to fulfillment. When he focused his attention on her clitoris, sucking on the sensitive nub and drawing it between his teeth to tug lightly, she flew apart with a cry of pleasure that echoed throughout the bedroom, the word *Snicklefritz* nothing more than a distant memory.

8

NICK LOVED WOMEN. He loved their sweet smell, their smooth skin, their silky hair. He especially loved pleasing them, hearing their soft moans and watching them buck and writhe as they came in his arms.

He'd had his share of women since he lost his virginity at sixteen to the captain of the varsity cheerleading squad under the bleachers in the gym. He liked sex, made no promises, and the women who were drawn to him had no problems with either fact. What they saw was what they got—a no-strings, footloose and fancy-free guy looking for a few laughs and a good time.

So why wasn't he laughing now?

Maybe it was the way Holly looked when she climaxed, eyes closed, breasts heaving, skin flushed and slick with sweat. Trusting. Not on display. He'd felt an unfamiliar pang in his chest when she'd called his name as he took her over the edge, shuddering beneath him. It sounded different coming from her than any other woman. Better.

Or maybe it was the way she was looking at him now. She'd opened her eyes and propped herself up on her elbows, staring at him with a dazed expression as he lay sprawled between her legs, his head resting on one creamy thigh. Her tongue ran the length of her lips and she swallowed as if she hadn't come in ages. Or ever.

"That was… I mean… I've never… Aaah!" She slumped back down and buried her head in the comforter.

He lifted his head, his chest swelling with pride. "You've never had an—"

"I most certainly have!" she cut him off, red-faced. "Just not…like that."

A devious grin spread across his face as he began a leisurely ascent up her leg to her rib cage. "Like what?" he teased.

"You—" She broke off, her breath hitching as he continued to travel upward, covering her body with his, her shirt and bra still bunched between them. He nuzzled his nose in the crook of her neck. She smelled like a woman should, not of some expensive perfume, but of soap and baby powder, clean and fresh. "You know what I mean. I've never had a man touch me…that way."

"Then you've been sleeping with the wrong men."

"You can say that again."

Not for the first time, Nick wondered what kind of a dickweed her ex was. He obviously hadn't given a crap about satisfying his wife's needs in the bedroom. Probably not anywhere else, either.

His loss, Nick thought, rolling to his back and reaching for the hem of his T-shirt.

But before he could lift it up and off, Holly surprised him by slipping out of her bra, pulling her blouse back up to her shoulders and climbing on top of him. He was tempted to ask why she didn't remove the damn shirt, too, but then she straddled his hips, pressing against his erection and short-circuiting his brain. "If I recall correctly, you promised me I could explore."

"Explore away," he croaked, lucky to manage even that with her sitting astride him.

She pushed his shirt up over his stomach. He raised

his head and shoulders, allowing her to tug it off. "Mmm. Yummy."

"I told you. I have food, baby. Ice cream."

"I like this better." She bent to press a kiss to the patch of hair between his nipples. Her hands roamed from his pecs to his abs and back again, making his muscles flex and his cock twitch hard in his jeans.

"Killing me..."

"Oh, my God, I'm sorry." She started to roll off him, but he caught her at the waist, stopping her.

"With pleasure, babe." He rocked against her so she could feel the hard length of his erection. "Killing me with pleasure."

"Oh." Her hands slid back down his torso, finding and settling on his belt buckle.

"Maybe I can die from it later."

"That wasn't exactly what I had in mind." She slid the buckle free and fingered the button on his jeans.

"Then I guess I'll have to lie back and take it like a man." He relaxed on the bed and crossed his arms behind his head, half anticipating and half dreading her sensual torture. It was his own damn fault, he knew. Hell, he'd practically given her a gold-engraved invitation with his whole equal-opportunity-seduction speech.

He could have her underneath him in seconds, his pants undone and his dick inside her before she even realized what was happening. And the little minx was tempting him to do just that, using her fingers, teeth and tongue to ramp him up to twelfth gear.

But then she lifted her head and her eyes met his, eagerness and indecision warring in their jade-green depths, and damned if he didn't want the eagerness to win out. Suddenly there wasn't a force on earth strong enough— not even his raging hard-on—to make him deprive her of the chance to give in to her desire and have her naughty way with him.

Holly's hands shook as she popped the button on his jeans and slowly—so damn slowly—pulled down the zipper. He sprang free, fully erect and completely bare. A drop of pre-come leaked from the slit. She dragged her eyes upward and raised an eyebrow at him. "Commando?"

He shrugged. "Tomorrow's laundry day."

"I didn't know big movie stars did their own laundry," she teased, brushing a finger over the head of his cock. It jerked in response and she drew back.

"This one does," he said, locking his fingers together in a superhuman effort to stop from grabbing her hand and putting it back where it sure as hell belonged. "If he wants clean clothes."

"Clothes are highly overrated. Clean or otherwise." She rose up on her knees and hovered over him for a long moment, her hands at his waistband but her eyes fixed on his chest.

He tried not to squirm like an overanxious schoolboy. "Like what you see?"

"Mmm-hmm." She licked her lips.

"Wanna see more?"

"Mmm-hmm." She tightened her hold on his waistband and took a deep breath as if steadying herself before making her next move, whatever that might be. He silently prayed that it involved the removal of his pants.

"Sometime today, maybe?"

"Mmm-hmm."

With a sharp tug, she yanked on his jeans. *Hallelujah!* He lifted his hips, helping her pull them off. Every muscle in his body tightened in anticipation as he watched her, her eyes so wide and aroused he just about came without another touch.

And then she reached down, encircling him with her fingers, and he was lost. Totally and completely lost. Slowly at first, with light, tentative movements, she stroked him, making his already rock-hard dick swell impossibly larger. Head back, he closed his eyes, letting the sensation of her hand working up and down his shaft, her thumb sweeping across the tip, wash over him.

"Is this… Am I…doing it right?"

Her nervousness, the awkward shyness mixed with obvious longing, did him in. He loved not knowing at any given moment which one would win out. Although he knew for damned sure which one he was rooting for. "If you do it any more right, I'm going to blow before I ever get inside you."

With his words she grew bolder, more sure of herself. Her pace increased, and he couldn't control the urge to thrust up into her fist. She closed her fingers more tightly around him and he moaned, knowing that he'd never forget this night, just as he'd never forgotten their kiss fifteen years ago.

Her movements stopped suddenly and he was about to protest when he felt the fine, soft ends of her hair tickle his thigh. "Can I…?" she breathed. "I want to taste you."

He knew what was coming next would probably be his undoing, but before he could stop her, her tongue was sliding around his crown, down his shaft and onto his balls, and finally her mouth, hot and tight, sucked him from root to tip.

He didn't think it was possible for things to get any hotter, but then—*sweet Jesus*—she hummed around him, a soft, mewling sound that had him a nanosecond away from losing control. A sweet thought, but he needed to be moving within her when he came.

"Baby, please…" He pulled from her mouth and she

let go with a loud *pop,* the sound echoing in the stillness of the bedroom.

"Nick?" She watched him, her eyes hazy and filled with confusion, as he moved her to one side, rolled off the bed and padded over to where she'd thrown his pants.

He pulled a condom from the back pocket and flipped it onto the bed.

"Always prepared. Are you sure you weren't a Boy Scout?"

"Hardly."

Her eyes softened and she reached out her hand. "Let me."

"Not if you want this to last." He ripped open the package and rolled the condom on. "And I don't know about you, sweetheart, but I'm nowhere near done yet."

He lay next to her, his erection hot, hard and demanding against her silky thigh. "You're beautiful, Holly." He took in her soft curves, her short dark hair fanned out across the pillow, her pale skin damp from their lovemaking. "So damn beautiful."

A pink flush crept up her cheeks and she tried to look away, but he stopped her, taking her chin and tilting her head toward him for a deep, soul-searching kiss. She wound her arms around his neck and kissed him back with a hunger that left him breathless and pretty much incapable of rational thought.

"Please, Nick," she whispered when they came up for air. "Take me. I can't wait any longer."

Neither could he.

He entered her in one swift, powerful thrust, her slick heat enveloping him. She sighed and hooked one leg over his hip, allowing him to slide in even farther.

"More."

With that one word, hoarse and needy, she shattered

what little remained of his self-control. He moved over her, his hands tangling in her hair, their mouths connecting as he drove into her like a storm pounding the shore. Claiming her. Drowning in her. She wrapped her legs around his waist, locking her ankles as if she'd never let go, and met him thrust for thrust, lifting her hips and taking everything he had.

He wished he could have her like this for hours, so perfect and pulsing underneath him. But he was close—so close—to letting go, and he could tell from her sexy little moans and the way her inner walls clenched around him that she was, too.

He eased his mouth from hers and slipped one hand between them, skimming it down through her soft, dark nest of curls until he found her clit. She cried out and arched off the bed, her head falling back and her hands sliding up his arms to grip his biceps. They were pressed so tightly together, and all that mattered was their race to the finish line, a race he was determined to lose.

"Don't hold back," he rasped as he stroked her. "Come with me, sweetheart."

That was all it took. With a shudder she was gone, screaming his name, her heels pressed into his back, her nails digging little half-moons into his arms. And he went right after her, exploding with the force of Mount St. Helens before collapsing on top of her and tucking his face into the curve of her neck.

"Nick, that was…"

"Yeah." There was so much more he wanted to say, but that was all he could manage without access to his brain.

He rolled over with her in his arms and she rested her head on his chest, her sweat-dampened hair tickling his chin. They lay like that for a few minutes as their breath-ing evened and their pounding hearts slowed until, finally, he felt her muscles go slack and she fell asleep.

9

THE PHONE shook Nick out of his stupor. No one had his apartment number yet but the front desk and his agent. "Damone," he mumbled into the receiver.

"I'll be there in fifteen. Just giving you the heads-up." Garrett sounded tired, too.

Nick rolled onto his back, alone in his big empty bed. He wanted Holly's naked ass pressed against his hip. Not only for some morning nookie—although that would have been good, too—but because…well, he didn't know why exactly. Because waking up alone this morning sucked when usually it left him feeling relieved.

He knew she was gone, had heard her quietly fumble her way out the door near dawn. It had taken every measure of self-control not to jump up and stop her. Escort her home. Take her to a diner for breakfast. Something.

But she'd said one night, and she'd meant it. Letting her leave on her own terms had felt right at the time.

Now it felt vaguely stupid.

"Nick. Are you there? Drunk?"

"Yes. And no." Staring at the ceiling, he pictured Holly moving over him. Shifting her weight every time he came close, to draw out his orgasm. And hers.

Fuck, she was hot.

"Just let me in when I get there, all right? Shit's happening."

"Right." Nick clicked off the phone. Nothing happening now could beat last night.

They'd made love three more times—once in the tiny pantry that served as a kitchen, where they got creative with the Ben & Jerry's, once in the bathroom, where they washed it off, and finally back in the bedroom. Each time had been better than the last.

Holly was incredible, open and passionate, with an innocent enthusiasm that more than made up for her lack of experience. And she was surprisingly funny. Nick was no stranger to hot sex, but she'd made him laugh as he never had before. Hell, he'd never known hot sex could be so damn much fun.

Only once did shy, nervous Holly reappear. They were in the kitchen, breaking out the ice cream. She looked so sexy wearing one of his T-shirts, the hem skimming her lush ass, and eating straight out of the carton. The sight of her tongue stealing out to lick the spoon made his cock stiffen and his brain cells turn to mush.

"You know what would make this taste even better," he said with a low growl when he couldn't stand any more.

"Sprinkles?" she suggested, her eyes twinkling.

"I was thinking more along the lines of this." He threw his spoon into the sink, hoisted her up onto the marble countertop and grabbed the bottom of her shirt, inching it away from her smooth thighs to her hips.

"Wait." She stopped him with a hand on his arm. Her eyes, wide and moist, reflected panic. Or doubt.

"Does this have anything to do with why you wanted the lights off earlier?" he asked softly.

She bowed her head, covering her eyes with her free hand. Slowly, carefully, he took her hand in his and lowered it to his chest, holding it there as he spoke. Her palm, still cool from the ice-cream container, chilled his bare skin, but he pressed it tighter against him, wanting her to feel the wild beat of his heart so she'd know just what she was doing to him. "Whatever you're hiding, it doesn't matter. It won't make you any less beautiful to me."

After a long pause, she raised her head and relinquished her grip on his arm. Then he lifted her shirt and understood.

He wanted to ask about the scars, ask what—or who— had hurt her so badly, but one look in her eyes told him she wasn't ready to go there. So instead, he slathered her with ice cream, licking and kissing and caressing her until she came so hard she would have fallen off the counter if he hadn't been there to catch her.

She returned the favor before they moved to the bathroom for soapy, slick shower sex, then back to the bed for exhausted, grinding, desperate sex. She'd been half-asleep when she fell on his chest after her last shaking orgasm. He'd held her there for an hour before she shifted to his side and curled around him, so soft and sweet.

And then she'd left.

Nick pulled on his jeans, not bothering to fasten them, and wandered through the apartment. Signs of her were everywhere, from the spoons in the sink to the seat down in the bathroom. It was almost like she'd stepped out to get them coffee and bagels.

But she wasn't coming back.

He'd just had the best sex of his life, with a woman he'd fantasized about for years. Who hadn't begged to stay the night, hadn't waited for the cameras to be ready at the door when she left, hadn't handed him a head shot and said they'd be great together on film. Holly should have been the perfect woman for him. After all, he was Nick

Damone, king of the fuck-and-run. Or, at his place, the fuck-and-hustle-her-out-the-door.

Except he hadn't brought a woman home in ages.

Couldn't remember the last time a woman he slept with hadn't asked for anything.

And he found the hangdog face staring out of the mirror a shock.

The front desk rang, and Nick gave the okay for Garrett to come up. Not ten seconds later his agent was knocking. The cocky bastard must've slipped past the concierge when he was on the phone.

"You look like shit." Garrett brushed past Nick and took up residence on the overstuffed couch.

"Thanks." Nick slammed the door shut, hastily doing up his jeans and sitting in one of the club chairs opposite Garrett. "Now tell me why you're here first thing in the morning on a Saturday."

"First you tell me. Who was she?"

"What she?"

"The she who kept you up all night. One of your L.A. bimbos? Or someone you met here in New York?"

"Not your business, as you know."

"Fine. I'm just saying. I tried to text you."

"Shit." Nick stalked into the bedroom and found his phone still in the pocket of his jacket, lying on the floor with the rest of his clothes. When he turned it on, he saw that he had a crap load of voice mails and texts, including at least six messages from Garrett.

"Are you serious?" He came back into the living room, cell phone open in his outstretched hand. "The show's back on?"

"Dead serious."

"They found another theater?" Nick couldn't hide the twinge of excitement in his voice, and not just because he'd be back on the boards. Sure, rehearsals had been better than he expected, even with all the bad luck and drama. But who was he kidding? That wasn't the reason his heart was doing the happy dance. Again. If the show was a go, he'd still be working with Holly. And while he was working *with* her, he could also be working *on* her.

"In a manner of speaking."

Nick sat on the arm of his chair and studied Garrett. This was how his agent delivered bad news, like when a costar quit and was replaced by some no-talent hack. Though in Malcolm's case the reverse would be true, so it couldn't be that. "What aren't you telling me?"

"I warned them." Garrett shuffled a few papers from his briefcase. "Said there was a good chance you'd walk. But it's the only option within fifty miles, and thanks to an unexpected hole in the schedule, rehearsals can start right away and the show can open in July as originally planned. So I brought the waivers and contracts for you to review and we can discuss—"

Nick rubbed his face. "Seriously, Garrett. Spit it out."

Garrett snapped his briefcase shut and set the papers down on the coffee table. "The Aaronsons have decided to do an out-of-town tryout. They're hoping for good reviews and a strong box office so they can move the show to Broadway when a venue opens. It's a limited run. Just a few weeks, then the show will either transfer or fold."

"Did you think I'd throw a tantrum over going to Jersey?"

"It's not Jersey, Nick."

"Chicago?" In recent years, the Windy City had seen the first bow of huge shows like *The Producers*, *Billy Elliot* and *Kinky Boots*.

"Nope."

The pinpricks on his neck told him what was coming next. And if it hadn't been for Holly, Nick would've ditched the show right there. Signed the waivers, found a new project and avoided the damn town like he'd been doing for years.

But leaving wasn't an option.

Not yet.

"The show's moving to the Elm City Repertory Theater. In—"

"New Haven." Nick completed the sentence for his friend, his tone flat and his mood grim. "I'm going home."

NOTHING IN STOCKTON ever seemed to change. Maneuvering her cart through the aisles of Gibson's Grocery, Holly could have closed her eyes and still grabbed the Parmesan, the pancake syrup and the Popsicles. Her eyes were open to check the list her mother had sent her with, written on a white envelope filled with ones and fives, but she needn't have bothered. Even the list didn't change.

"Hello, sunshine."

"Hey there, Earl." Holly approached the meat counter, confident that the shop owner and butcher would already know her order.

"The usual?"

"Mmm-hmm. But double it up."

"Ah." His biggest grin yet. "All you kids back in town?"

"Just three of us. Ivy's in Florida." Sunday dinner was always an event at the Nelson homestead, and her mom had coerced Noelle and Gabe, their brother, to make the two-hour trek north from the city. Ivy, Gabe's twin, was in Miami for the week, working on a spread for *Cosmopolitan.* She'd been cryptic about who she was shooting, which meant it was probably a hot, famous actor.

If Holly didn't know better, she'd think it was Nick.

Nick.

Holly cracked her neck, trying to stay awake. She didn't usually mind coming home, despite the grilling she knew she'd face at dinner. It was a nice break from city life. But today she felt more naughty than nice, her lack of sleep punishing and her muscles outraged. Nick might be used to hour after hour of acrobatic lovemaking, but last night had been Holly's first experience in sexual gymnastics and her thighs were screaming that they'd never recover.

Nick.

After leaving his place—okay, turning tail like a coward—Holly had grabbed her purse, phone and a change of clothes and headed north to avoid any awkwardness. She didn't want to dish the dirt with Devin, or sit pathetically waiting for a phone call or flower delivery when that was never part of the deal.

Halfway home she'd gotten the news about the Elm City Rep and been knotted with tension ever since. It was great—hometown support would be incredible, and it was a brilliant publicity move—but she didn't know how Nick would handle the possibility of seeing his father.

Or seeing Holly, for that matter. She wasn't so sure she wouldn't drop to her knees before the man involuntarily. He was a sex god, and her legs were still weak from the pleasure.

"Did you say something, Holly?"

"Uh, no." Holly bolted awake. Had she? "I'm a little tired. Must've zoned out there for a minute."

Earl gave her a concerned look. "Sounded like 'nick,' or maybe 'lick.' You need ice cream? Aisle…"

Her face began to boil. "Four. Yeah, thanks." She shot off.

"Don't forget your order." He rushed around the counter and dropped three tightly wrapped white packages into her cart.

"Right. Thanks, Earl." At the last moment, she lifted onto her toes to give him a kiss.

With his face red, too, she felt better. She was whistling her way to the register when she veered off the list. Chips and guacamole were her specialty. As she ran back to the produce section, a child's laugh, followed by the thump of falling boxes, stopped her in her tracks.

"Balloon!"

A towheaded little boy sat surrounded by the remains of a cereal display, babbling happily and pointing at a Mylar caricature of a tiger floating above the rubble. He looked to be about two years old, the same age as...

"Balloon," he repeated, struggling to regain his footing on chubby toddler legs. Holly thought she might cry as she watched him, his blue eyes filled with wonder as he reached for the string of the balloon.

She scanned the aisle. No mother. No father. No responsible adult in sight.

Except her.

Blinking back tears, she set down her basket and scooped up the little boy, who had one foot on the bottom shelf of the display in his quest for the balloon. "Easy there, partner. You're going to get yourself hurt."

"Balloon?" His eyes widened and his lower lip quivered.

"No, sweetie." She tightened her hold on the squirming toddler. He was soft and sweet and smelled of talcum powder and milk, and her heart felt like it was about to shatter into a million pieces. "No balloon today. We have to find your mommy or daddy."

"Mommy?" His lip trembled again and his eyes watered. Holly braced for a full-blown meltdown. Instead, the little boy's face broke into a toothy grin at the sight of a woman about Holly's age with hair as blond as his, racing toward them down the aisle. "Mommy!"

"There you are, Brendan." She stretched out her arms to her son. "Mommy was so worried about you."

Holly handed the boy over to her, savoring one last whiff of talcum and milk. "He's fine. He just wanted a closer look at that tiger." She gestured to the balloon.

"Oh, no." The woman frowned at the pile of cereal boxes. "Did he make this mess? I swear, I only turned my back for a second."

"Fast, aren't they?" Holly knelt and started picking up the boxes, thankful for the distraction.

"Here, let me help." The woman went to set her son down, but Holly stopped her. "It's okay. I've got it."

"Thank you." The woman hitched the boy higher on her hip. "For everything."

With a little wave she turned and headed back the way she came before Holly could even choke out a "you're welcome."

Holly picked up her basket, paid for her groceries and loaded them in her VW Bug. She sat for a few minutes, her head resting against the steering wheel, still shaking from her encounter with Brendan and his mother. She thought after almost two years the empty feeling would go away. And it did. Sometimes. For a while. Only to come back to haunt her when she heard a child laugh. Or call for "Mommy." Or when she saw a family walking hand in hand.

She lifted her head and stared at herself in the rearview mirror. Her hair was matted down from where she'd laid on the steering wheel, and her face was chalky, all traces of the minimal lipstick and blush she'd applied earlier long gone. God, she looked like crap.

It had to stop, this falling apart whenever she saw or heard a child. It was the only way she'd have a chance at a future, a family. Holly wasn't naive—or stupid—enough to think that an average Jane like her would fit into the world of a big-time move star like Nick as more than a fling. That was why she had promised herself to stick to the one-night-only deal. She needed a nice, safe, stable guy. The kind of guy Clark had started off being, before he'd lost his job and spiraled down into a cesspool of alcoholism and depression.

With one last, long sigh, Holly pulled herself together. She was about to back out of the parking space when her phone rang. "Hi, Mom," she answered with a false gaiety she hoped her usually all-knowing mother would fail to detect. "You've got mayo, right? I'm going to make some guacamole."

"I'm not sure guacamole goes with my braciole and *succu.*"

Perfect. Another thing she screwed up.

"It's an appetizer, Mom. It goes with anything."

"Fine, *cara.* I hope you bought enough to make plenty. We have some unexpected guests today."

"Let me guess. Cade?"

"Naturally. Although, as Gabe's best friend, he's hardly unexpected, is he?"

"And Mr. Bauermann?" Their elderly neighbor, a recent widower, was a frequent guest.

"That's two."

"You mean there's more?"

"Just one. I ran into him outside Maude's. The poor man was going to have dinner there. Now, I don't mean to insult Maude's cooking. It's perfectly serviceable. But Sunday dinner? In a diner? It's criminal."

"What poor man?"

"You know him, *cara.*"

Oh, God. Her mother. The ultimate drama queen. She'd draw this out as long as humanly possible.

Holly's phone beeped, sparing her from having to listen to her mother's spiel. "Mom, I have to go. Devin's on the other line. She's keeping an eye on my apartment for me while I'm gone. I'll be there in a few minutes and I've got enough for everyone."

Less than fifteen minutes and a short conversation with Devin later, Holly passed the familiar weather-beaten Grower's Paradise sign. It marked the entrance to the long gravel driveway leading to the Nelson house and the nursery and gardens beyond. Parking, she recognized Gabe's Land Rover and Noelle's Mini Cooper but not the unfamiliar silver Audi S6 sandwiched between them.

"Hey, guys," she called, the screen door banging shut behind her. "I'm home." She set the groceries on the counter and knelt to pet Jasper, the orange tabby she'd found abandoned as a kitten. The cat gave her his traditional greeting, weaving around her legs. "Where is everyone?"

"Back here," a voice answered. It sounded like Gabe but was too muffled for her to be sure. "On the porch."

Abandoning the cat, she made her way through the house she'd grown up in, the familiar smells of lemon wax, fresh-baked bread and her mother's sauce simmering on the stove welcoming her home. "Hey there, baby brother."

She stepped onto the veranda that spanned the back of the house. "Long time no—"

The end of her sentence died in her throat.

Gabe's short, neat, almost military haircut was a far cry from the thick, tousled locks on the man standing in front of her. And although at around six-one Gabe was considered fairly tall, he was a good three inches shorter than the giant on the porch.

"Nick." Her voice wavered, betraying her.

"In the flesh." His eyes lifted, then dropped the length of her body. "Surprised?"

She drew herself up, ignoring the skip of her heart at his heated appraisal. "That's putting it mildly."

10

Judging from the look on her face, he figured he had about five seconds to explain himself before she lost it.

"Holly, I—"

"Why are you here? You're supposed to be in New York. And what have you done with my family?"

Make that three seconds.

Nick shifted his feet, then forced them still. He could do cool-and-distant in his sleep. "They're in the greenhouse. Your father's showing off a hybrid rose."

"The New Dawn?" She started for the porch steps, but he blocked her, stepping between the two pillars that framed the stairway.

"I stayed behind to see you. We need to talk."

"About what?"

"About us."

"There is no us."

"There could be."

"One night, Nick. One. *Uno. Ein.*"

"I can count."

"Prove it."

He leaned against one post, head cocked, arms crossed. His mouth quirked into a subtle half smile. "Why are you so dead set against an encore? It sure seemed like you were enjoying yourself. Unless all that screaming and moaning was just—"

"Would you pipe down, for God's sake?" she hissed under her breath, scanning the yard. "My family will be back any minute. And the last thing I want is for them to know that we... You know. They think I'm enough of a screw-up already."

Great. She considered their night together a mistake. Another first for him. He straightened, fists clenched, his whole body, which was relaxed a heartbeat ago, radiating tension. She raised a hand to her throat as she took a step back from him.

Damn. He hadn't meant to frighten her. Someone had sure as hell done a number on her to make her so skittish. Probably her ex, Nick thought, remembering those scars and wondering not for the first time how much of Holly's play was autobiographical. He had a sudden and overwhelming desire to find the bastard and beat the motherloving crap out of him. Instead, he made a conscious effort to loosen up and soften his voice when he spoke next.

"I can be professional about this."

"Really? Had a lot of practice with sex on set?" She spun on her heel and headed back into the house.

"Last I checked, my bedroom's not a movie set," he called, following her. "Neither is my kitchen. Or my bathroom."

"Whatever. I can be professional, too. Or however you act after recreational sex."

Recreational sex? Who talked like that?

His sweet little bookworm/playwright/sex kitten, who probably hadn't ever had a one-night stand.

Until him.

It was kind of adorable watching her try to act worldly. It made him want to spin her around and kiss her until she melted like butter in a hot frying pan. The way she had when he'd first kissed her back in high school. But that wasn't likely, seeing as how she was royally pissed at him for showing up and throwing a monkey wrench into her carefully constructed one-night-only plan.

She grabbed a knife and began eviscerating a poor avocado with quick, sure strokes. He sat a safe distance away from her at the oversize farm table that dominated the room. "We're going to be working together. Don't you think we should…?"

"No." The rhythmic slap-slapping of her knife against the cutting board added extra emphasis to her denial. "We shouldn't."

He leaned back in his chair, balancing on two legs. "You don't—"

Slap.

"—even know—"

Slap.

"—what I was going—"

Slap.

"—to suggest."

Slap.

"I've got a pretty good idea." She exchanged the knife for a spoon and began scooping the meat from the avocado into a glass bowl.

"Do you?" He shifted his weight, dropping the front legs of the chair back onto the floor. They landed with a *thwack* on the tile, making Holly flinch.

She continued scooping as if he hadn't spoken.

"Earth to Holly…"

She turned to face him, bracing her hands against the counter behind her. "Look, Nick. I'm only going to say this once, so listen close. We had sex."

The corner of his mouth curled. "A lot of sex."

"And it was great."

"Really great." His smile widened.

"But it can't happen again, no matter how much we both want it to. I won't let it."

We'll see about that. Out loud he said, "Agreed."

She tilted her chin to look up at him, all five feet three inches of her bristling with righteous indignation. He liked that about her, her feistiness. She reminded him of Tinker Bell, with an attitude. "Fine."

He took a step closer, meeting her challenge. "Fine."

"I—"

The screen door slammed and footsteps tromped toward the kitchen, leaving whatever she'd been about to say stuck in her throat.

"Hey, Holls, you in there?" called a female voice.

"Come see the New Dawn. It's beautiful," her father added.

"Mom said you're making guacamole. I hope you didn't forget the onion like last time. It's nowhere near as good without the onion."

Nick stepped back and leaned against the counter, keeping his distance from Holly as her family descended on her like a swarm of locusts. Loud, love-starved locusts. He watched, his chest feeling as if someone had parked a Humvee on it, as they laughed and hugged, talking over one another. So this was how a family was supposed to behave. Who knew?

Sundays at his house had been spent alone, hiding in his bedroom, listening to his father get progressively drunker, progressively louder, progressively meaner. Back then, he'd wish he was old enough and strong enough to protect his mother, or that she was strong enough to protect herself. And him.

Nick looked away.

"Everything all right?" Holly's father stood slightly apart from the group, his voice quiet but firm. He might have been talking to his daughter but his eyes were locked on Nick. Clearly, Nick hadn't moved away from his little girl far or fast enough. He remembered Nils Nelson as a large, jovial man, the logical choice to play Santa Claus every year in the Stockton holiday parade. There wasn't a damned thing jolly about him now.

"Oh, Nils. Stop scowling." Elena Nelson gave Nick a smile that seemed to spread throughout her tiny frame. At least someone was happy to have him there. "Nick is our guest. I'm sure he and Holly were just talking shop."

"Uh, yeah." Holly pasted a polite smile on her face and went back to preparing her guacamole. "Talking shop."

"You two must have lots to discuss." Noelle took a seat at the table and shot Nick a grin that was both reassuring and apologetic at the same time. "Since you get to keep working together."

"Where's Cade?" Holly's attempt to change the subject was about as subtle as a kick to the groin.

"Next door getting Mr. Bauermann." Gabe went to stick a finger in the guacamole and Holly slapped it away.

"They'll be here any minute." Elena made a shooing motion with her hands. "Now out, all of you, or I'll never get dinner on the table."

HOLLY HAD SAT through many a Nelson Sunday supper. The fatty food. The constant questions. The mostly good-natured ribbing. She thought she'd seen—and survived—it all.

She was wrong. Nothing could have prepared her for the humiliation of having her worst moments replayed for Nick Damone.

"Remember when Holly tried to rescue that poor squirrel with the broken leg?"

"The one she kept in a box under her bed?"

"Yeah, until it chewed its way out. Stupid rodent terrorized us for three days before Dad caught it."

"How about her unforgettable performance as Muff Potter in the Stockton Elementary School's production of *Tom Sawyer?*"

"You mean when the seat of her pants split open in front of the entire student body? Who could forget that?"

"The sight of her Strawberry Shortcake underwear scarred those kids for life."

"See what you missed, Nick, not moving here until high school?"

She was going to kill them. One by one. Slowly and painfully.

"Stop embarrassing your sister." Holly's mother spooned a heaping serving of pasta onto her husband's plate. "You too, Cade."

Sufficiently chastised, the Three Amigos ate in silence for a few minutes, the only sound in the cavernous farmhouse kitchen the clanking of forks and knives.

It was too good to last.

"So, Holly." Noelle, twirling a single strand of spaghetti around her fork, was the first to start in on her again. Did she ever eat? "Seeing anyone special?"

Holly almost choked on one of her mother's super-secret-recipe meatballs. Her eyes flicked to Nick, sitting next to her, naturally, huge and hot and devastatingly handsome. He was no help at all, acting all strong and silent as he dug into his plate of pasta and braciole. She had half a mind to grab the fire extinguisher from the hall closet and hose him down. Then again, maybe it'd be better to turn it on herself and cool off her own raging hormones.

"That's a good question." When he finally spoke it was low enough that only she could hear. She hoped. "One I'd sure like to know the answer to."

What the heck was he playing at? Her parents were eyeing them suspiciously. Her sister looked like the proverbial cat that swallowed the canary. Gabe and Cade, her self-appointed protectors, sat tightly coiled, ready to pounce on Nick if he laid so much as a finger on her. Only Mr. Bauermann, trying to stab an especially elusive meatball with his fork, seemed completely oblivious to the sexual energy in the room.

She had to give them some sort of response, if only to keep the boys from messing up Nick's pretty face. "I wish. But you know what it's like getting a show off the ground. No time for anything else. Certainly not a relationship."

"I'm not so sure about that," Noelle countered. "Every production has its share of showmances. It's inevitable. People thrown together in close quarters for hours on end." She pinned her gaze on Nick from across the table. "Right, Nick?"

"I guess," he agreed with a shrug. "But that's not my style. Usually."

"What about you, Noe? Are you still dating that... Erp!" Holly jerked with a squeal as Nick's warm fingers slid up her thigh and under her skirt, his movements hidden by the long tablecloth. What on earth had possessed her to dress for dinner anyway?

"You all right?" her brother asked. "Cade's a firefighter. I'm pretty sure he knows the Heimlich maneuver."

"Sure do."

"Hiccups," she said through gritted teeth, glancing sideways at Nick. The good-for-nothing jerk had the nerve to sit there smiling at her family with an innocent expression worthy of a choirboy, all the while creeping his fingers higher and higher until he was almost touching the hem of her undies. She said a silent prayer of thanks that she'd gone with one of the new thongs her sister had made her buy on their recent pre-Nick shopping spree instead of her traditional granny panties, then gave herself a mental slap across the face. What difference did her choice of underwear make? Nick Damone was not getting in her pants again. No way, no how.

"What do you think you're doing?" she whispered through clenched teeth, pressing her knees together and putting a hand over his, stopping its upward trajectory.

He turned his choirboy charm on her. "Me? Not a thing. I'm the picture of virtue."

Only if virtue looks like sex on a stick. She pressed her legs tighter and tried her hardest to focus on what her sister was saying from across the table instead of the heat generated by Nick's hand under it.

"You know who I'd like to have a showmance with? Ryan Gosling." Noelle sucked a strand of spaghetti into her mouth, eyeing Nick over her fork. "Can you introduce me to him?"

"How about Jennifer Lawrence?" Gabe chimed in. "Do you know her?"

"Basta." Elena shushed them with a flick of her wrist. "What did I warn you? No pestering Niccolò about his famous friends. We're going to have a nice, normal Sunday dinner."

Gabe snorted. "Since when have our Sunday dinners been nice and normal? Right, Holls?"

"I...uh..."

She was saved from getting dragged into that battle by a shrill, persistent beeping.

"That's me." Cade stood, unclipping his pager from his

belt and checking the screen. "Sorry. Got to call in. Can I use your phone? It's more reliable than my cell out here."

"Of course. Why don't you use the one in Dad's office. It'll be quieter there." Holly waved off her mother, who had started to rise, and jumped up, pushing her chair back.

"Uh, it's okay," Cade said, moving to the door. "I know where it is. Thanks." His footsteps echoed down the hall.

"So eager to get away from me?" The hand that had been on Holly's leg reached for his wine glass. So why was her thigh still tingling?

"It's your own fault," she hissed. "For not following our agreement."

"What agreement?" He sipped his merlot.

"You know," she whispered, sneaking furtive glances at her family, thankfully otherwise engaged in capellini and conversation. "No… You know."

"Oh. Forgot. Sorry."

"I'll bet."

"You're not gonna believe this." Cade stormed back into the room, grabbing a couple of rolls from a basket on the table and stuffing them in his pockets.

"Believe what?" Noelle asked, smacking Cade's hand as he reached for another roll.

"The fire marshal wants me to meet him at the Rep ASAP."

Holly's stomach plummeted. The temperature in the room seemed to drop, too, and everyone—including Mr. Bauermann—stopped eating. Without the clatter of silverware the kitchen was eerily silent.

"Oh, God," she moaned. "Please don't tell me it burned down, too."

"Not yet. And not ever, if we can help it."

Nick threw down his napkin and frowned. "What's that supposed to mean?"

"We just got word from the NYFD. The fire that destroyed the Deville was arson."

_11_

ARSON. SHIT.

"They're sure?" Nick rubbed a hand across his jaw, the short, crisp hairs of his beard scratching his palm.

Cade nodded. "Positive. There were traces of gasoline on the floor. And they dug out what was left of the starter."

"Starter?" Holly slumped back into her chair. One look at her ashen face made Nick want to wrap her in his arms, the watchful eyes of her family be damned.

"The arsonist wedged a lit cigarette with a rubber band wrapped around the end into a matchbook," Cade explained. "By the time the matches ignited and started the fire, he was probably miles away."

"Okay. So the fire was set. What does that have to do with the Rep?" This from logical, lawyerly Gabe. The guy had always been the voice of reason, even in high school. He was practically cross-examining Cade now. Thank God, because Nick's brain was fuzzy and tired.

"The NYFD said something about other suspicious accidents during preproduction."

"Oh, my God." Holly gripped the edge of the table. "The food poisoning. And the power outage."

Nick groaned, remembering his conversation with Marisa at Pearl. "And the bomb threat that grounded Marisa's flight in Canada."

The show was cursed. That's what everyone kept saying. He wasn't a superstitious person, so he hadn't gone along with that crap. But why hadn't he suspected foul play? There were too many incidents for it to be a coincidence.

He knew why. Because the delays had worked in his favor. More time with Holly.

And more danger. Idiot.

"Food poisoning? Bomb threats?" Holly's mother pushed away her half-full plate. "Why haven't we heard about this?"

"Maybe we should take this outside," Nick suggested, seeing the pinched looks on her parents' faces.

Cade shook his head. "No time. I've got to run. Fire marshal's waiting."

Holly rose and picked up her plate, crossing to the sink. "I'm coming with you."

"No can do. An arson investigation team's on its way up from New York. No one's going near the Rep or the company housing until we give the all-clear."

"How long's that going to take?" Nick asked.

"Not sure. A few days, at least."

"A few days?" Holly's plate clattered into the sink.

"Maybe a week. There's a lot of ground to cover. The theater itself. All the rooms for the cast and crew."

"A week?" Nick could hear the panic in her voice. "But the rest of the company's supposed to be here tomorrow." He could almost see the wheels turning in her head. Losing a day or two of rehearsal would suck, but they'd make up for lost time. A whole week would be a disaster. Anything more than that and folks would start to jump ship, finding work with other shows.

Although that wouldn't be such a bad thing where Malcolm was concerned....

"Tell them to stay put. Everything's on hold while we sweep the place. We'll work as fast as we can." Evading Noelle's ever-ready hand, Cade grabbed another roll.

"I'll let you know as soon as we've got a more definite time frame," he called over his shoulder, sprinting out of the room.

Nick drew his brows together, wrinkling his forehead. "Where does that leave us?"

"You can always head back to the city," Gabe suggested. "Or hang out up here with your family."

Like that was going to happen.

"I'll stay here, if it's okay with you guys." Holly looked from one parent to the other. "I can work on the script changes the producers asked for. And I'm sure Dad won't mind a little help with the nursery, right?"

Nils gave what Nick interpreted as an affirmative grunt.

Then again, maybe hanging out in Stockton wasn't such a bad idea, after all. He could play bodyguard, keep an eye on Holly and make sure nothing happened to her. And maybe while he was at it, convince her to give him a second chance.

"And I'll bet Ethan can have the PR people get started on some promotional stuff," she continued, biting her lip and drumming her fingers on her thigh. Sexy little schemer. "You know, TV appearances, radio interviews, speaking engagements. Play up the hometown-girl-makes-good angle. If I'm going to be in town, I might as well do something useful."

Yes!

Just like when he was on the gridiron in high school, Nick saw an opening and went for it. "I'd be happy to stay and help with that. The Aaronsons chose New Haven because we both grew up here, right? But I can't bunk with my parents."

He had to come up with an excuse. Fast. Holly might suspect his relationship with his family was less than ideal, but he wasn't about to admit that in front of the rest of the Brady Bunch. His personal life was just that—personal. "They're, uh, having some work done on the house."

He was at the fifty-yard line....

"What about the Charter Oak Inn?" Gabe suggested. The bed-and-breakfast was the only game in Stockton when it came to lodging.

Noelle shook her head. "No room."

The forty...

"Seriously?" Holly scowled at her sister.

"The whole place is booked all week for some wedding."

The thirty...

"Sorry, Nick," Holly said. Only, she didn't sound all that sorry. Didn't look sorry, either. More like relieved. "But there're plenty of hotels in New Haven. I'm sure Ted and Judith will put you up in one of them."

"Don't be silly," her mother cut in. "Why would he stay in a cold, impersonal hotel room when he can stay with us. We have plenty of room. And three home-cooked meals a day. You can't get that in any hotel."

The twenty...

"I'll be good." At what, Nick didn't say, although several possibilities sprang to mind. All of which involved making her come. Multiple times. "Promise. You'll hardly know I'm here."

Unless, of course, he was giving her those orgasms, in which case she'd be screaming his name. "Besides, didn't you say your dad could use an extra hand around here?"

Nils grunted again, which Nick took as another yes.

The ten...

She narrowed her eyes at him. "You realize that would entail getting your hands dirty, right?"

"Hey, I wasn't always a movie star. I've done my share of manual labor."

The five…

Emotions passed across Holly's face in quick succession: anger, fear, something that looked suspiciously like arousal and, finally, resignation. Nick reminded himself to tell her not to play poker—unless it was a private game of strip poker with him.

"Okay, you win. Stay here, if it'll make you happy."

Touchdown!

He leaned back in his chair and flashed her a grin worthy of the village idiot. "Oh, it'll make me happy, all right. And Ted and Judith, too. The last thing they need is to fork out any more money than they have to."

"You can have my old room," Noelle offered.

"Or mine," Gabe put in. "If you prefer debate trophies and sports equipment to toe shoes and New Kids on the Block posters."

"Please," Noelle scoffed. "I took those down ages ago. It's 'N Sync now."

"Thanks, man." Nick turned to Holly's parents. "You, too, Mr. and Mrs. Nelson."

"Of course, *Niccolò.*" Elena stood and began to clear the table, shooting a scathing glance at Holly. "I'm sure I speak for *all* of us when I say we're happy to have you here, for as long as necessary."

THE LAST THING Holly wanted to do was show their new guest to his temporary digs. But as her mother said, she spoke for *all* the Nelsons, and when she'd offered Holly's services as tour guide there was no room for objection.

"Follow me." Holly started up the stairs that led to the

bedrooms. She knew what she'd find behind Gabe's door. Her mother had kept each of the Nelson siblings' rooms as virtual shrines, and his was no exception. Debate trophies displayed on a shelf above his desk, organized by height and evenly spaced. Patriots and Red Sox pennants hanging over the dresser. A baseball, bat and glove resting in one corner, giving the room a faint smell of leather that mixed with the lemon Pledge her mother sprayed like pixie dust over every surface.

Everything in its place. Including the enormous four-poster bed.

Even the word brought on a flood of erotic images. Nick's head between her legs, his soft, dark hair tickling her thighs, his tongue teasing her into a mindless frenzy. His body covering hers, her soft curves melding with his hard edges. And his hands—oh, those hands—molding her breasts, sliding down her rib cage, gripping her hips...

She stopped and clutched the banister, determined to banish the memories—the desires—from her brain. She'd had her night with Nick. There wasn't going to be another.

What kind of fool played around with a guy as hot—and smart and talented and rich and famous—as Nick, knowing they'd likely end up with third-degree emotional burns when he left?

Not newly self-protective Holly, who didn't act on impulse and regret it forever.

Not newly launched, career-minded Holly, who needed to be taken seriously as a writer.

Not newly respectable daughter Holly, who wasn't going to have sex in her brother's room.

She'd just have to stay far, far away from that bed. Or any bed, for that matter, when Nick was around. And countertops. And bathtubs. To be safe, she should probably add couches, futons and oversize chairs to that list.

She was halfway up the staircase before she registered the lack of footsteps behind her. She swiveled her head to find Nick still standing at the foot of the stairs, looking like a *GQ* model with one hand in his pocket and the other on the strap of the duffel slung over his shoulder.

"Problem?"

"Just enjoying the view." He rested one foot on the bottom step, scanning her body with his eyes. Was it her imagination or did they linger on her backside?

"Is this your idea of being good?" She wasn't going to survive even a day of him, never mind a whole week. Silently, she prayed Cade and the fire marshal would make quick work of their investigation so she and Nick wouldn't have to live under the same roof for long.

One corner of Nick's mouth curled into a devilish grin. "From where I stand, things look very, very good."

"You know what I mean. You said I wouldn't even know you were here."

He shrugged. "I lied."

"Typical." And exactly what she was afraid of with Nick. He might not lie intentionally, but he'd lie to himself that what they had was special enough to last for more than the run of the show. He must know better. His whole adult life had been a series of beautiful women who went as fast as they came, his fly-by-night relationships documented and catalogued by a dozen websites.

Not that she'd been searching him on Google. She didn't need more than one source for her gossip, and now that she was home she could steal her mother's *People* as soon as it arrived. It was going to be up to her to keep herself out of the tabloids. Just one shot of him kissing her, followed a few weeks later by one of him leaving her, would shatter her. Everyone in town would know she'd been played. She didn't have Noelle's poise or Gabe's confidence, or even Ivy's don't-give-a-shit outlook on life. There'd be no shaking it off for her.

She'd have to become a hermit, just when her life was starting to get fun.

No way.

Her protective armor fully in place, she made her stand at the top of the stairs.

"Come on." She took off down the hall. "Gabe's room's the third door on the left. You can put your stuff in there."

"Hold up." Nick shot up the staircase. "Your mom promised me an escort."

"Are you always this difficult?"

"Only when I know I'm right." He stepped closer, angling his head to study her through hooded eyes. A habit of his, she'd noticed. One that had her swooning into his neck for a drag of his cologne before she regained control.

"And what exactly are you right about?"

"You and me." He moved even nearer. *Crap.* If her family saw them like this, she'd never hear the end of it.

With a sigh, she pushed open the door to Gabe's room and ducked inside. Better to take her stand there, in private. If she humiliated herself it wouldn't be witnessed by anyone but Nick. "Here it is. Home, sweet home. For the time being."

Nick paused at the threshold and looked down the hall. "Where's your room?"

"Wouldn't you like to know."

"Yeah. That's why I asked."

"Let's just say it's too close to my parents' room for you to get any ideas." Holly surveyed the room. Everything was exactly as she'd expected, from the trophies to the lemon Pledge.

"I've already got plenty of ideas, sweetheart." Nick

came in, depositing his bag on the bed. The room shrank by yards.

"Excuse me." Gabe poked his head in the door and cleared his throat. "I hate to interrupt your verbal fore-play…"

Holly dissolved into a fit of coughing, which Nick stemmed by reaching around and patting her on the back.

"…but I'm heading back to the city. I'm in the Special Victims Unit now, but I've got a buddy with Violent Crimes. I'll see what I can find out about the fire from him."

"Thanks." Holly crossed to Gabe and gave him a quick hug. "I always knew having a big-shot district attorney for a baby brother would come in handy someday. I just thought it would be for stuff like fixing traffic tickets."

"I hate to ask," Gabe began, pulling back and studying Holly's face intently, "but do you think…maybe…your ex is behind all this?"

"Clark?" she whispered. "But he's…out of state."

"He could be working with an accomplice. And he's got a pretty strong motive for closing the show down."

"Not to mention a criminal record," Holly muttered low enough so that Nick, searching for something in his duffel, wouldn't hear. She hoped.

"Don't worry, Holls," Gabe reassured her. "Whoever's doing this, he's targeting the show, not you. You'll be safe here with Mom and Dad."

"And me," Nick added, abandoning his search and taking a step toward them. If she hadn't been so freaked out about the whole arson thing, Holly would have laughed at the way he puffed out his chest, like an overeager adolescent trying to impress his best girl.

His girl.

Gabe gave her another fast squeeze before heading for

the door. He stopped when he reached Nick and looked him straight in the eye, a serious expression on his face. "If she gets hurt, it's on you, man."

Nick nodded, meeting his gaze. "Not going to happen."

"Hello?" Holly's voice was laced with sarcasm. "Still here. And fully capable of taking care of myself." Except for her heart.

"Try to stay out of trouble."

With a wave of his hand, Gabe was gone, leaving Nick and Holly alone, within striking distance of that big, beautiful bed.

What was it Gabe had said? Stay out of trouble?

Some things, Holly thought, were easier said than done.

12

Holly swore under her breath as she fumbled in her darkened bedroom for her muck boots. What had she been thinking when she volunteered for the morning shift at the nursery? No civilized human being should be required to rise before the sun.

Of course, her father was probably already dressed and in the greenhouse, watering the perennials. At sixty-six, he had more energy than most thirty-somethings.

Including Nick, Holly thought, her outstretched hand finally coming into contact with the cool rubber of one of her boots. She felt around for the other, grabbed the pair and crept in her stocking feet out of the room and down the long, dark hall. Sure, Nick had offered to help. But she didn't think he'd appreciate being dragged out of bed in the wee hours on his first full day in Stockton. Seeing his muscles bunch and flex as he mulched the gardens would have made it worth hauling her own sorry butt up at such an ungodly hour, though. If she followed the look-don't-touch rule, she'd be fine, or so she told herself. Right before she considered what crimes she'd commit—theoretically—to see the man in shorts and work boots. Shirtless, with a thin sheen of sweat covering his chest and back.

A soft thump and the pitter-patter of furry feet told her Jasper had jumped off her bed and was fast catching up to her. His fluffy shadow approached, his purr vibrating through Holly's toes. "Hey there, big fella," she cooed. "Ready to catch some mice?"

With a haughty tilt of his white-tinged chin that seemed to say "as if," the tabby snubbed her and glided past. Rearing up on his hind legs, he stretched his front paws toward the door handle of Gabe's room. Nick lay sleeping in there, wearing who knew how much—or how little.

"Jasper, no," she hissed, a corner of her brain dimly recalling Nick's casual comment at dinner about his cat allergy. She should have warned him that Jasper was a regular feline Houdini, able to open doors. "Down."

Neither "no" nor "down" had any effect on the cat. Holly dropped her boots and started after him, but before she could grab the little bugger he had pressed on the handle and thrown his considerable weight against the door, pushing it open. With his tail held high and an air of superiority befitting his Egyptian ancestors, he squeezed through, leaving Holly staring after him.

Damn, double damn and triple damn.

She had two choices. Keep going down the hall as if nothing had happened. Or rescue Nick from a trip to the E.R. for a shot of Benadryl.

"Stupid cat." Her choice made, she inched the door open farther. She'd sneak in, grab the beast and sneak out. Easy peasy lemon squeezy.

Light crept through the half-open curtains, and the faint smell of freshly mown grass drifted through the open window. And on the bed...

Holly's breath hitched at the sight of Nick sprawled, one long leg hanging off the mattress. He wasn't naked, thanks to a pair of formfitting boxer briefs—*drat*—but his muscled chest and legs were bare, the sheet bunched around his ankles, as if he'd been too spent after a bout of

down-and-dirty, muss-the-covers action to bother pulling it up. He looked every inch the Hollywood bad boy
the press made him out to be, even in sleep, with his light
scruff, deep tan and sculpted-for-IMAX body. But at the
same time, he appeared surprisingly vulnerable, his eyes
closed, long dark lashes resting against his cheeks, his
strong jaw relaxed, his breathing deep and even.

She'd seen plenty of him that night in his apartment, but
in her rush to leave she'd never had the chance to study him
undetected. Now, with him prostrate and unconscious, she
could appreciate the perfect symmetry of his face, cheek
over chin next to perfectly angled nose. The chiseled highs
and lows of his pecs and abs. Corded forearms leading to
thick wrists and strong, long-fingered hands. She itched
to touch. Taste. Smell. Curl up next to him and bask in the
heat radiating off his body.

He's just a man, she told herself, exhaling quietly in
a futile effort to slow her racing heart. Flesh, blood and
bone, like any other.

*But oh, what a delectable combination of flesh, blood
and bone.*

She took a tentative step toward him before remembering what she was there for. Jasper. Where was that
darned cat?

Holly scanned the room and found him coiled at the
foot of the bed, ready to spring onto Nick's outstretched
legs. "C'mere, Jasper," she pleaded softly. "Come on, boy.
I saw some Manchego cheese in the refrigerator. Your favorite." He might be lower on the evolutionary scale, but
he sure had expensive taste in treats.

Unmoved by the bribe, the cat leaped with unexpected
ease onto the bed, landing inches from Nick's pillow. With
a swish of his tail, the cat circled a few times before settling into the crook of Nick's arm, his cocky orange head

tucked under Nick's chin and one paw extended across his sculpted rib cage.

Lucky cat.

Holly held her breath, waiting for Nick to stir. But the guy slept like a stone. She tiptoed to the bedside and reached for the cat, ignoring the devil on her shoulder telling her to oh so casually brush against Nick as she did. She had to get Jasper out of there before Nick's allergies kicked in. She couldn't imagine anything more humiliating than him waking up sneezing and finding her gawking at him like one of his obsessed fangirls. Not exactly how she'd planned to start her day.

"That's it, boy," she crooned softly, getting close enough to graze his soft fur with her fingertips. "Just a little bit farther and we'll go get some of that nice overpriced cheese…."

"Any farther and I won't be responsible for what happens next."

Holly jumped back at the sound of Nick's voice, deep and gravelly and early-morning sexy. The movement startled Jasper, who dived off the bed with a form worthy of Greg Louganis and stalked out of the room. Not that Holly blamed him. She'd be pretty upset, too, if someone got between her and a nearly naked Nick.

"Don't get me wrong," Nick rumbled, interrupting her thoughts. He raised himself up on one elbow and pinned her with those velvet eyes. "I'm certainly not complaining. It's not every day a guy wakes up to a pair of beautiful breasts in his face."

"Hey," she retorted, crossing her arms in front of her chest to hide the fact that her nipples were threatening to poke holes through her top. "It was my breasts or the cat's butt."

He rolled to his back and stretched, making the muscles

of his chest and arms ripple. "I definitely got the better end of that bargain."

"Don't get used to it." She swallowed, her mouth dry. The man was even more lethal in the predawn hours, with his hair all mussed and his eyes sultry and heavy-lidded. "I'm not planning on getting you up like this every morning."

He shifted his hips to one side. "I'm sure I can come up with some alternative but equally enjoyable ways for you to…get me up."

"Pig." She grabbed a pillow from the floor and tossed it at him.

He grinned and deflected it easily. "I was talking about breakfast in bed. Soft music. Shiatsu. You're the one with your mind in the gutter."

"Dream on. This is a landscaping and garden center, not Club Med. And since you're up, you might as well be useful."

"I can be useful." He swung out of bed and stretched again, sending her heart rate into overdrive. "Very, very useful."

"How about you put on some clothes so we can get to work?"

"I've got a better idea." In two steps he reached her, one hand snaking around her back to draw her to him, the other tugging her flannel work shirt from her jeans. "How about you take off some clothes so we can play?"

He slipped his hand under her shirt, letting it travel slowly up her rib cage until it cupped her breast, his thumb grazing her nipple through the cool satin of her bra.

"I… We…can't."

"Give me one good reason why not." His voice dropped even lower and he leaned in to tease the tender flesh of her earlobe with his lips, making every nerve ending in her body buzz.

"I'll give you two." She fixed her eyes on a poster of David Ortiz over Nick's shoulder. It was that or bury her face in his chest and breathe in that warm, sleepy, sexy smell that was totally Nick, totally irresistible. "My parents."

"So we'll be quiet. I'm up for the challenge." His lips traveled down her neck to her collarbone and she sagged a little against him. "Are you?"

"I… Oh." She broke off on a low, lingering moan when he nudged the collar of her shirt aside and nipped her shoulder, then followed it with a soothing kiss.

"That's it." He smiled against her skin. "Let go."

Something bumped the back of her thigh and Holly realized he'd backed her up against Gabe's desk. She put a palm down to steady herself and heard the clatter of one of Gabe's trophies falling to the floor.

"Shh." He nudged one leg between hers, sandwiching her between the desk and his hot, hard, not-quite-naked body. His lips continued their torture, his warm breath fanning her neck as he spoke. "Remember. Parents. Quiet."

"I'm not sure I can stay silent when you do that."

"Do what?" His thumb brushed her nipple and she moaned.

"That."

"Yes." He lifted his head and she whimpered at the sudden loss of his mouth. "You can. Let me do this. Let me please you."

With an almost inaudible groan, he kissed her. It wasn't so much a kiss as a question, an invitation for Holly to accept or deny. He started slow, outlining her bottom lip with his tongue for a long, agonizing moment, then finally letting his mouth settle over hers.

It was an invitation she couldn't refuse.

Holly threw her arms around his waist and threw herself into the kiss, any thought of resisting him obliterated by the slick slide of his tongue on hers, the rasp of his thumb on her nipple, the press of his growing erection against her hip. Kissing him was like Christmas, Mardi Gras and a good hair day, all rolled into one.

He abandoned her breast and slid his hand down to the waistband of her jeans, popping the button free and lowering the zipper. She widened her legs, allowing his fingers to dip inside her panties. She was throbbing as he teased and taunted, coming close to her swollen clit but never touching it.

She pried her mouth from his, panting. "Nick, please."

"Please what?" He plunged the tip of one finger between her wet folds then withdrew it, leaving her breathless and needy.

"You know what. Stop messing around." She reached for him through his boxers. "I want you inside me."

"I want that, too, sweetheart." He thrust into her hand. "Do you feel how hard I am? But ladies first."

He circled her entrance one last, torturous time before working two fingers inside. She arched her back and pushed against his hand.

"That's right, baby. I know you need it. Take it." He flicked his thumb over her clit as he continued to move inside her, bringing her to the brink.

Her head dropped back and she grabbed onto his arms, her nails digging into his biceps. "Oh, God, Nick. I'm going to come."

His fingers slowed. "Just remember. Quiet, Holly. No one can know. You're in control."

She swallowed hard and nodded.

"Good. Now look at me. And come."

He resumed his movements, fingers pumping in and out, his maddening thumb teasing her with the skill of a virtuoso. Her eyes widened and she came in a heated rush, burying her face in his chest to drown her cries.

Nick withdrew his fingers, wrapped his arms around her and held her, leaning down to brush a soft kiss across her temple. "You're trembling."

"Give me a minute." She breathed him in. Warm. Sexy. Nick. "It'll stop. I hope."

"It's okay. I love seeing you like this. Watching you come apart. Knowing I'm the one who got you there."

A knock at the door, followed by her mother's voice, made both of them startle. "Are you up, *Niccolò?* I thought I heard voices."

Damn. So much for whispering. Her stomach clenched like a guilty teenager, caught with her pants down. Or open. Not that she'd been the kind of kid to sneak a guy over. That was Noelle's territory. Holly was what her sister would call a late bloomer.

She prodded Nick, mutely urging him to respond. "Uh, yeah, I'm up, Mrs. Nelson." He scrambled for his jeans, lying in a heap on the floor, while Holly cowered near the most convenient hiding place—the closet—refastening her own pants and straightening her shirt. "Just, um, talking to my agent on the phone."

"Isn't it a little early for a business call?"

"You haven't met Garrett. The man doesn't sleep."

"As long as you're up you might as well come downstairs and have some breakfast. I made pancakes and sausage."

"That sounds great. I'll be right down."

"Oh, and have you seen Holly? Her father could use some help outside."

Double damn. She shot Nick a panicked look. He appeared equally dumbstruck, and she said a silent prayer for him to call on his acting chops to deliver a convincing lie.

"Um, no, I'm, uh, still in bed. But I'd be happy to pitch in. Just give me a few minutes to get dressed."

"That's very sweet of you, *Niccolò*. Now hurry and come eat before it gets cold."

Her mother's footsteps retreated and Holly slumped against the dresser, breathing a sigh of relief before turning to Nick. "Seriously? Twenty million a picture and that's the best you could come up with?"

He shrugged on a Van Halen T-shirt. "What can I say? Improvisation was never one of my strengths. But I more than make up for it in…other areas."

Holly blushed at the reminder that barely seconds ago he was giving her one of the best orgasms of her life, while she was almost fully clothed. One heated glance from Nick and her look-don't-touch rule, along with her ability to form coherent thought, had flown out the window.

Not again. If she was going to survive this whole experience with her heart intact, she needed to set some boundaries. And the best way to do that was to stay as far away from Nick as possible until the theater reopened and they could get back to business. It wouldn't be easy when they were sharing the same house, but it was necessary, seeing as she had the willpower of a vampire in a blood bank when it came to him.

"I've got to get downstairs before my father sends out a search party." She smoothed her hair and crossed to the door, hoping her swollen lips and flushed cheeks wouldn't give her away to her parents. "Are you coming?"

Too late, she realized the huge opening she'd given him. "Not this morning, apparently." With a wolfish grin, he adjusted himself and zipped up his jeans, following her out of the room. "But I'll take a rain check."

IT WASN'T EASY to woo a girl when you were ankle-deep in cow manure. Or was it horseshit? Whatever. All Nick knew was that a week that had started off great had turned to crap. Figuratively and literally.

He'd barely seen Holly in the two days since that morning when she and the tata twins had given him that spectacular wake-up call. Oh, sure, they had meals together, along with her parents. And he'd caught her peeking at him when he was working outside with her dad in the afternoon, when the sun was high and he'd taken his shirt off to beat the heat. But time alone together? Nada. She was back to her avoidance strategy, and the woman was harder to pin down than a casting director during pilot season.

"You about finished there, Niklas?" Holly's father rounded the corner of the greenhouse, startling Nick back into motion with the fertilizer.

"Yes, sir." Nick bent and scooped up a shovel full of compost from the wheelbarrow next to him. Anything to avoid facing the father of the woman he'd been picturing naked, a man so well-mannered and respectful he insisted on calling Nick by his full name in Swedish. "This is the last bed."

"Head on up to the house when you're done. Elena's made fried chicken and potato salad for lunch."

"Will do." Nick spread the mixture around a Dr. Seuss–looking plant with a tall, thorny stalk and clusters of purple berries that Nils had called devil's-walking-stick. He turned to shovel up another load.

"And make sure you find Holly. She's been looking for you."

Nick paused in midshovel. Holly? Looking for him? But before he could ask why, her father had disappeared, leaving as quickly as he'd come.

He finished in record time, anxious to get back to the

house and find out what Holly wanted with him. Had she heard from Ethan? Was the theater cleared? Or maybe there'd been another "incident." Good or bad, it had to be something to do with the show. She'd made it clear she wasn't interested in any more between-the-sheets action.

Not that that was going to stop him from trying.

She was in the kitchen getting lunch on the table when he found her. Her hair was shoved under a weather-beaten Red Sox cap and she wore no makeup. An apron over her usual work outfit—jeans and a faded flannel shirt—proclaimed her Too Hot to Handle.

Damned if she wasn't.

"You wanted me?" he asked, making his way over to the sink to wash his hands.

Her cheeks reddened, letting him know she hadn't missed the double meaning. "In a manner of speaking."

She set down a huge platter of chicken in the center of the table. His stomach grumbled, reminding him that it had been hours since he'd eaten breakfast. He grabbed for a chicken leg and she smacked his still-damp hand away. "What gives?"

"Change of plans for this afternoon." She took off her apron and hung it on a hook by the refrigerator. "You're off the grunt patrol."

"I can't say I'm not grateful." Nick rolled his shoulders back and tipped his head from side to side, trying to soothe his sore muscles. He hadn't been lying when he'd told her he was no stranger to manual labor, but it had been a while, and landscaping was damn hard work. A lot more demanding than waiting tables or bartending, his primary modes of support before he'd struck gold with Trent Savage. "But why?"

She plucked a piece of chicken from the platter and bit into it, humming softly in appreciation. A rivulet of juice dribbled down her chin and she wiped it away with the back of her hand before answering him. He found it hard to focus on what she was saying.

Jesus Christ. What the hell was wrong with him? He was used to having silicone-enhanced actresses throw themselves at him, whom he could fend off with one hand tied behind his back. But one innocent, food-induced moan from Holly, and he was a goner.

Somehow her words broke through his lust-filled haze. "We're going back to school."

13

FROM THE WINGS, Mr. Traver cleared his throat to get Nick's attention and tapped the face of his watch.

"Looks like we have time for one last question." Nick glanced at Holly, sitting on the auditorium stage next to him in a molded-plastic chair identical to the one he occupied, for confirmation. She shrugged and nodded her head as if to say, *Go ahead. This one's all yours.* He surveyed the sea of shining, eager faces and raised hands in his former teacher's Intro to Drama class, finally settling on a skinny boy with an unfortunate cowlick who looked like a blond Harry Potter.

"Third row. Blue shirt. Glasses."

"Me?" the boy squeaked.

"Yes. What's your name?"

"It's Kevin, sir."

"And what's your question, Kevin?"

"I wanted to know…" He tugged at his collar. "The way you've described it, your role in this play is, like, so different from your movies. And from you, unless, I mean, assuming you're not, like, a wife-beater or anything."

The class tittered and one boy in the back row not so discreetly coughed "loser" into his hand. Mr. Traver poked his head out from behind one of the curtain legs, but Nick waved him off. "I think I know where you're going with this, Kevin. But I'd like to hear the rest of your question, if it's all right with the peanut gallery."

The cougher squirmed in his seat, and a beaming Kevin continued, "How do you, like, identify with a character who's such a scumbag?"

"So, basically, how much does it suck being the bad guy after years of playing the hero?" The class laughed again, this time with Nick instead of at Kevin. "In all seriousness, that's a good question, one it took me a long time to figure out. Every actor's process is different. For me, it's about digging deep, finding something redeeming about the character beneath the ugly surface. No one's black-and-white, all good or all bad. Although I'll admit the good's buried deeper in some than others."

Like Holly's ex. And his father.

"How about you, Ms. Ryan?" a girl piped up from behind Kevin. "Why'd you write about domestic violence?"

Shit. Nick figured the last thing Holly wanted to talk about was how close to home this play hit for her. "Sorry, but I think we're out of time, guys. Thanks for—"

"It's okay," Holly said, surprising him. He was even more shocked to see her on the edge of her chair, light dancing in her green eyes and looking almost giddy with anticipation. "*The Lesser Vessel* isn't just about spousal abuse. It's about making what you think is the right choice—the safe choice—and having it turn out horribly wrong. It's about having the judgment to recognize you've made a mistake and the courage to make it right. And I think that's something we all experience at some point in our lives."

"Kind of like pulling a U-ie?" a smart-ass in a red hoodie yelled.

Holly found the boy slinking in his seat and nailed him

with her gaze. He slumped even farther and pulled his hood down over his face.

Attagirl.

"More like making amends, if they're due, then starting over. And getting it right this time." She opened her mouth as if to say more, then shut it, nodding a little to herself.

She was right. She'd said it all.

"On that note," Mr. Traver interrupted, joining them onstage, "time to wrap up." His eyes darted from Nick to Holly and back again. "Any parting words of advice for these budding thespians?"

"I think Nick's better equipped to answer that question than I am," Holly said, biting her lip, probably as amused by Mr. Traver's formality as Nick was. Another thing about good old Stockton that hadn't changed in fifteen years.

"Oh, I wouldn't say that." Nick gave Holly a knowing smile and turned his attention to the class. "The best advice I ever got came from the woman sitting next to me. When no one else believed in me, when I was afraid to believe in myself, she told me this—be bold, be brave." Out of the corner of his eye he saw Holly stiffen. "And she was right. In this business, you need to leave your fear at the stage door and make daring choices, in and out of the audition room."

Almost as if it had been choreographed, the bell rang, drowning out his last word. The students rushed to crowd around Nick, snapping photos on cell phones. Many had playbills, posters and pictures for him to sign. A few even asked for Holly's autograph, but mostly she watched as Nick handled the hubbub with his typical, easygoing charm, posing with the kids and whipping out a black Sharpie from his pocket, scrawling his barely legible movie-star signature on whatever they threw at him.

"Your *Our Town* reflections are due on Monday," Mr.

Traver reminded them. "And auditions for *Noises Off* will be Tuesday and Wednesday after school, with callbacks on Thursday. Sign-up sheet is on the Thespian Society board in the activities center."

"We'd better get out of here," Nick said when the door had closed behind the last student. "Those pics will be all over the internet soon. And I think I saw one kid recording the whole thing."

"Thank them for keeping it on the down low until we were done," Holly told the teacher. "I know the PR department has some stuff planned for us, but this was for the kids. I didn't want it to become a media circus."

"And we meant what we said earlier," Nick added. "We'd love to have you and your students as our guests at a performance. The box office will call you and set it up."

A few more thank-yous and hugs later, and Nick's and Holly's footsteps echoed down the school corridor. "I'd almost forgotten," Nick muttered as they rounded the corner at the end of the hall.

"Forgotten what?"

"How it feels to create something from nothing. To tell stories and express yourself." He slowed so she could catch up to him. Another hazard of his height. "All the reasons I wanted to act in the first place. Those kids, their questions…"

Holly came up beside him, nodding. "Yeah. When that girl asked why I wrote about domestic violence…"

"I thought that might make you…uncomfortable." He still wasn't sure how much of Holly's play was autobiographical. Oh, he'd gathered from her veiled remarks that her ex was a real prick. But had he actually done all the shit Nick's character did in the play? His jaw clenched.

"It did," she admitted, her arm brushing his as they walked side by side. His anger was gone as fast as it had come, replaced by desire. "A little. But it also made me remember why I started writing. And why I wrote *The Lesser Vessel*. I was kind of dreading the Aaronsons' revisions, but now I feel…"

"Rejuvenated?"

"And you said you didn't know any big words." She nudged him playfully with her elbow and he nudged her back, smiling. She made him feel comfortable, at ease, free to be Nick Damone, regular guy, and not Nick Damone, movie star. It was a feeling he liked. A feeling he could get used to.

Never in a million years when he'd walked these halls as a dumb kid would he have imagined the pleasures life had in store for him. But Holly made him believe there was more to come. And come. And…

"But you're right," she was saying. "That's exactly how I feel. I want to rush home and lock myself in my room with my laptop."

Not quite what he had in mind. Sure, talking with the kids had re-energized him, too. But he was also horny. His brain whirred, trying to figure out another plan—one that ended with them naked, sticky and sated. "First we have to celebrate."

"Celebrate what?"

"Our mutual rejuvenation."

"What did you have in mind?" she asked, her tone wary. "Wait, let me guess. Does it involve you, me and skinny-dipping in Leffert's Pond?"

"No." Although that wasn't a half-bad idea. He'd have to catalogue it for later. "It involves you, me and ice cream."

She blushed, and he knew she was remembering their creative use of Ben & Jerry's.

"It's not what you think," he continued, dropping his

voice to a whisper. "Not that I'd object to a repeat of our Cherry Garcia experiment. This time with sprinkles."

If possible, she blushed even deeper, and he had to jam his hands in his pockets to stop himself from reaching out and running a finger down one beautifully flushed cheek. "But I was thinking more along the lines of the Scoop Shop."

The Scoop, as it was known by the locals, had been a Stockton hot spot for as long as anyone could remember. Nick had taken many a girl there after seeing a movie at the Regal. Or before making out at Hotchkiss Point.

None of those girls had been Holly, though, a situation he intended to remedy.

"I don't know. I really need to get started on those script changes."

"We can stop for a quick cone. Or maybe share a Scoop split." He felt the telltale pressure of his hardening cock against his zipper as he imagined feeding her the ice-cream stand's signature dessert, her full, pouting lips closing around the spoon, her tongue darting out to catch a stray dab of whipped cream. "I'll even let you have the cherry."

"No, thanks." She shook her head. "I'm watching my girlish figure."

Me, too, he thought.

"Aw, c'mon. Have pity on me." He shot her his best you-know-you-can't-resist-me smile and threw in a dose of puppy-dog eyes for good measure. "I've been a good boy, haven't I? Working with your dad. Setting the table for your mom."

"What do you want? A medal?"

What he wanted was for her to race him to the car, leap over the center console and ride him like a pogo stick to orgasm town. But since that was out of the question, he'd settle for ice cream. For now.

"I deserve some kind of reward."

"Fine. But we're getting it to go."

"Works for me." He pulled a baseball cap from his back pocket and jammed it on his head, making sure the brim was low enough to obscure his face. The Stockton locals had been great about giving him space, but he couldn't be too careful. With a hand at the small of her back, he steered Holly toward the exit. His brain was spinning off again, running through the list of remote locations where he could take her to enjoy their dessert, in private.

"Nick, wait." They had reached the car, but she stopped him from opening her door, a soft, imploring hand on his arm. "What you said in there. You know, about the advice thing. I had no idea…"

"That I remembered?" She nodded and averted her eyes, looking everywhere but at him. "Of course I do," he assured her. "I remember everything about that night."

He slid a finger under her chin and tipped it up so that she had no choice but to meet his gaze. Her eyes, wide and shining, stared into his, making his chest constrict and his next word come out on a rush of air. "Everything."

Risking his luck, he dipped his head to steal a quick kiss. His lips were only a hairsbreadth from hers when he caught a glimpse of a Volvo station wagon pulling into the parking lot. Dark blue, with a magnetic sign on the door advertising All-American Realty: Click or Call, We Do It All and a phone number underneath.

The car was new, but he remembered that sign. Hated that fucking sign. Do It All, his ass. More like Screw It All Up.

The Volvo parked across from his Audi. Nick pulled back from a confused Holly and braced himself, stance wide, hands jammed into his pockets, for the confrontation he'd been dreading since Garrett had dropped the bombshell that the show was transferring to New Haven.

His lips tightened into a thin line as an older couple got out. The man, almost as tall as Nick and with the same strong, sharp features, helped the smaller, more delicate woman out of the car, one hand at her elbow and the other clutching a bulky file.

At first glance, they looked like the poster couple for marital bliss. But Nick's practiced eye saw the unyielding, possessive grip on her arm, the nervous tapping of her foot, the way her red-rimmed eyes darted from left to right, never settling on anything or anyone.

Until her sharp intake of breath told Nick those eyes had landed on him.

"Nicky!" She took a step toward him, her reed-thin legs trembling, then looked to her husband, still holding fast to her elbow, as if for permission to continue.

Nick took off the cap, stuffed it in his pocket and sighed, hands clenched into fists behind his back. Another thing in Stockton that hadn't changed. Not that he'd expected it to.

"Hey, Mom." He gave her a warm smile, then turned to address the man he hadn't spoken to in well over a decade, his voice sharp enough to cut steel. "Dad."

14

A FEW MINUTES ago Nick had been almost happy-go-lucky, tossing out sexual double entendres like beads at a Mardi Gras parade. Reeling her in with an almost kiss that had promised to melt her body, claim her heart and steal her soul.

Now he was as tight as a coiled spring, his whole body rigid, his normally warm brown eyes stony and his lips, usually so kissably full, compressed into a thin, harsh line. A muscle ticked on his jaw, making her want to reach out and smooth his tension away.

From what Nick had told her in choppy mini-sentences, she'd guessed his relationship with his parents—especially his father—was strained. But this went way beyond strained. Nick was a bomb waiting to explode.

"Mom. It's nice to see you." Voice low and dangerous, his hand skimmed from Holly's neck to the small of her back, gripping the thin fabric of her dress as if it was his fingerhold on a cliff. "You may know Holly. Her family owns Grower's Paradise. She wrote the play I'm working on now."

"Oh." Nick's mother flushed with what looked like pleasure. As if she received affection so rarely she wanted to wrap it up with a ribbon and paste it in a scrapbook.

If Holly had to guess, she hadn't seen her son in a really, really long time.

Mrs. Damone held out her hand. "So lovely to—"

Nick's father tugged his wife's hand down before Holly could untangle her own from her sundress pocket. "We have to get these contracts inside, Vera."

"We can stay and chat a few minutes, can't we, Sal?" The older woman placed a trembling palm on her husband's arm, but he shook it off. "It's been so long...."

"A few minutes can mean the difference between a sale and walking away empty-handed in this business."

"Please, Sal. Just five minutes. He's your son...."

"I meant what I said when he walked out on his scholarship and on us." Sal might have been talking to his wife, but his eyes were riveted on Nick. "I don't have a son. Not anymore. And neither do you."

"I didn't walk out." The ticking muscle in Nick's jaw seemed to pick up speed. "You threw me out. Right after you threw me against the wall."

Holly focused on breathing. Long, slow, quiet breaths. She didn't want to let Nick know how much his father reminded her of Clark, making her skin prickle and her insides twist. From the fingernails digging into her spine, she could tell Nick was barely holding on as it was. The last thing he needed was a panic-stricken female at his side.

Eyes forward, she willed herself. *Keep smiling. No sudden movements.* She wanted to throw her arms around him and shout, "It's not your fault." She knew that. Did he? Some people were just assholes, even if they were related to you.

She knew that, too.

"Please." The word was probably a permanent staple in Nick's mother's vocabulary. It had been in Holly's for the

last few years of her marriage. "Not like this. Not here."
She scanned the parking lot, empty of witnesses.

Holly also glanced around for paparazzi in the surrounding trees. Their school visit had been last-minute
and hush-hush, but she wouldn't put it past the gossip rags
to have someone on Nick's tail. Even if they didn't, it'd
been almost ten minutes since they'd left Mr. Traver and
his cell-phone-carrying, Instagram-happy students. Plenty
of time for the local news stations to send a crew over. A
money shot of Nick punching his father would be a complete nightmare for him, personally and professionally.

She could feel Nick's fingers curling against her back-
bone. A second later they relaxed and he released her,
smoothing the dress against her bottom and giving it a pat,
as if he'd decided not to up the asshole ante.

Nick sighed, rubbing the back of his neck. "It's okay,
Mom. I'll be in town for six weeks. I promise we'll get
together. Maybe you can spend some time at the theater,
see me at work."

"You call that work?" Nick's father almost spat the last
word. "Being a spoiled movie star? Prancing around a
stage like a fairy? Talk to me about work when you've
got a few calluses."

"Hey." Holly let go of Nick's arm and took a step forward. So much for no sudden movements. How dare he
belittle their work? She came chin-to-chest on the man,
but she took on his ice-blue stare. "Nick does not prance."

"Don't bother." Nick tugged her back a step and laced
his hand in hers, firm and still. Only his racing pulse told
the real story. "It's not worth it. He's not worth it. Besides,
I'll take prancing onstage over throwing a fucking piece of
pigskin five hundred times a day, then hearing over dinner how every goddamn throw was wrong."

His father stepped neatly past Nick, ignoring every

word. "Let's go, Vera. I'm late for my meeting and we need this sale."

His mother tearfully brushed Nick with a kiss as she passed by, and he offered a diluted version of his million-dollar smile that didn't come close to reaching his eyes. "Sorry, Mom."

"I know you are, Nicky."

"I'll call you."

"You always do, honey. I love you. And your father meant well. You loved football..."

"Save it, Mom."

"Vera."

"It's wonderful to see you, Nicky," his mother whispered. "And you, too, Holly."

Manners observed, she slipped her thin, wrinkled hand from Nick's shoulder and shuffled away, head down, leaving Holly and Nick to stare after her as she followed in her husband's wake.

"She thinks she loves the bastard," Nick said quietly a few moments later.

"Yeah." Holly sighed. She got that.

He lifted Holly's hand to his lips and gave it a small, warm kiss just as the Channel 8 mobile news van pulled into the parking lot. "Let's get the fuck out of here."

"HOLLY?"

Nick shifted uncomfortably in his seat, and not just because no matter how far back he slid the damn thing his right knee kept hitting the steering column. They'd been driving in relative silence for the past ten minutes, the only break in the awkward stillness an occasional sniffle from Holly's side of the car. Or was she hiccuping? He couldn't really tell, and he was too chicken to risk a glance her way to find out.

"Are you okay?" he ventured.

More silence. Then another sob. Or hiccup. Or whatever.

There was no way he was taking her home like this. He made the split-second decision to turn onto the narrow, bumpy road that circled Leffert's Pond, not knowing exactly where he was going but thankful for the swells and ruts that required his full attention, distracting him from the crying—or hiccuping—or whatever-ing—woman in the next seat.

He hadn't had much experience sticking around for the aftermath of his father's abuse, physical or otherwise. When he was younger, his mother had hustled him off to his room. By the time he was in his teens, he'd gotten smart enough to get out without any prompting once the storm had died down and he knew his mom was safe.

He cringed as Holly let out another unidentifiable sound. Better not to mention that things could have gone a whole lot worse. He was a little relieved, actually. His father had always been a fan of the surprise attack—aka the sucker punch. That would have sent things in an entirely different direction altogether.

Nick unclenched his fingers around the wheel. He'd bitten his tongue back there, and it'd been hard as hell. He waited for some revelation about what to do with Holly. Was she having a flashback?

Jesus.

This was why he liked scripts and make-believe. The drama in real life hurt too damn much.

Then he saw it. The for-sale sign in front of a familiar gray clapboard house. The scene of the crime, so to speak. Not that kissing Holly had been a crime, although Jessie Pagano should have been hauled off in handcuffs for interrupting them.

The driveway was empty, the lawn overgrown. He took it as an omen and swung a hard left into the drive, spraying gravel as he braked.

Then he manned up and looked at her.

Shit.

Holly sat hunched over, her bent head resting on crossed arms. Yet somehow she still managed to be alluring. Maybe it was the graceful curve of her back, her soft, pale skin visible between the straps of her sundress. Or the long line of her exposed neck, calling for him to lick a moist trail from her hairline to her collarbone.

She drew a deep, shaky breath and he mentally slapped himself for being a complete and total horndog. Trembling, she pressed her palms deep into her eye sockets. But it wasn't enough to stop the flood of tears running down her beautiful face.

Ouch.

Nick hadn't cried since he was kid, another lesson his father had drilled into him.

His chest seized, high and tight at the memory. It was how he'd brace for a hit on the field, or at home. Now he used that instinct for stunts. His trainer called it his wall of muscle, which looked great on film. That wall made one thing a safe bet: no one was going to gut punch him again.

Ever.

"Hey, come on. Don't cry." He gave her an awkward pat on the back. Christ, he sucked at this emotional hand-holding stuff. "You were great back there. Defending my honor."

She lifted her head to look at him and his chest squeezed even tighter. A wet finger snaked its way into his clenched hand, resting on his thigh. "That sucked."

"Just an average day for me and my father." He lifted his other hand from her back and brushed a tear from her cheek, one corner of his mouth involuntarily twisting into a smile. "I've had to deal with my parents' bullshit my whole life. I'm just sorry you had to see it."

"You know what?" Unfastening her seat belt, Holly leaned back, stretched her legs and gave a long, shuddering sigh. "I'm not."

"You're not?"

"Nope. In fact, the more I think about it, the more I think it's exactly what I needed to see."

"How so?"

"A part of me has always wondered if I made the right decision leaving when I did. If it would have turned out… differently if I had stayed and tried to work things out with Clark." She bit her lip and stared out the window. "Now I know."

"Trust me. There's no working things out with some guys. My father's one of them. From what you've told me, I'm pretty sure your ex is another."

"Yeah. I guess you and I have more in common than I thought, with men like that in our pasts." Holly closed her eyes and stretched again, arching her back and raising her hands over her head. The movement made her breasts strain against the thin fabric of her dress, and suddenly the atmosphere in the car seemed stifling, claustrophobic.

Nick dropped his hand and surreptitiously adjusted his cargo shorts so she wouldn't see the havoc she was wreaking on his libido. What was the matter with him? If he didn't get the hell out of that car—and fast—he was going to take her right there in the driveway, which, he reminded himself, would be a colossal mistake. *Hello*—not two minutes ago she was a hot sniffling mess, thanks to his father and the memories of her piece-of-shit ex-husband he'd dredged up. Definitely not the time to go all alpha on her.

"Come on." He flung open the driver's door. "Let's fin-

ish this discussion outside. I need some air." He climbed
out and headed through the tall grass toward the lake.

"Where are we going?" The sound of crunching gravel
morphed into the swish of the grass against her ankles as
she got out of the car and trailed after him.

"Back to where it all began."

15

HOLLY WAS HALFWAY to the lake, letting the cool breeze off the water calm her jangling nerves, when she saw the dock and stopped short.

Even faded and warping, it was still the showpiece of Leffert's Pond. A long series of boards led to a large square platform covered by what looked like the roof of a Chinese pagoda. A wooden dinghy bobbed alongside, tied to one of the pilings.

Give her a thousand covered docks and Holly would still recognize this one. Nick's words echoed in her head.

Back to where it all began.

He stood under the Paganos' ostentatious pagoda, in almost the same spot where he'd found her the night of the cast party. Facing the water, hands thrust into the pockets of his shorts, he looked like a modern-day pirate. The wind ruffled his dark curls, dangerous and sexy, as he stood surveying his plot of the briny deep.

She made her way across the yard and down the dock. It creaked and swayed with every step, signaling her approach, but he didn't turn, not even when she reached his side. "Are you sure we should be here?"

He angled his head and his chocolate eyes mirrored hers, half-lost in memory. When he spoke, his voice was low and rough, sending ripples down her spine. "I can't think of anyplace better. Can you?"

"You know what I mean. It's private property."

"You must have missed the sign out front. It's on the market. And from the looks of things, it's been vacant for a while. No one around to bother us."

She'd been too puffy-eyed to spot the sign when they pulled in, but the traces of neglect were evident in the cracked wood pilings and peeling paint. It was eerie how, despite the changes, the place still felt so familiar. And a little bit "theirs."

The pier was New England rustic, and the lapping water relaxed her. Nick was right. This was just what she needed.

"Thanks for bringing me here. It's beautiful. And thanks for not freaking out back in the car. I'm sorry I lost it like that...."

"Hey, it's okay. My fucked-up family has that effect on people." Nick lowered his long, lean frame to sit on the dock, and held a hand up to her.

Relaxed or not, her emotions were still running high. Any physical contact and she might spontaneously combust. She wiped a damp hand on her backside and sat beside him, not touching. "I hope you don't expect any words of wisdom this time. I'm fresh out."

"You sure?" He reached down and dragged his hand through the water. The simple movement made his biceps ripple, and she bit back a sigh. The man was beautiful, even in the middle of a personal crisis. "You did so well last time."

"Right. So well your father doesn't speak to you and you barely see your mother."

"My father was never going to be satisfied with me, no matter what I did. And my mother was never going to stand up to him. I was trapped, and you gave me a way out. At least this way I'm following my own dream, not his."

"I wouldn't give up on your mom. Not just yet."

"How'd you work up the courage to leave?"

Holly shook her head and stared out across the surface of the lake, clear and calm and dappled by the late-afternoon sunlight. "It had nothing to do with courage and everything to do with necessity."

"Bullshit."

"How do you know that?"

"Because I know you. Even at sixteen, you had the courage to be your own person, not who your parents, or your teachers, or your friends expected you to be. I envied that."

She stared down at the cool, clear water swirling around the pilings. Even now, as a grown woman, it was hard for her to hear a compliment. She let her legs dangle off the dock next to his, taking care not to brush against him. Something restless was building inside her and she needed to keep it locked away. Touching Nick seemed to burst her wide open, and it was hard to concentrate with the heat from his body surrounding her, making the hairs on her arm stand at attention. "I'm still in shock that you remember our conversation at the cast party. Now I'm supposed to believe you were jealous of me, too?"

"I told you, I remember everything." Nick reached for her hand but she slid it out of range and under her thigh. "And not just about that night. About you. You always brought lunch from home, either peanut butter and jelly or tuna salad. And you ate with the band geek—uh, the music department kids, at a table in the corner by the vending machines. Your favorite subject was history, especially ancient civilizations. You even dressed as Cleopatra one Halloween."

"Helen of Troy," Holly muttered, amazed he'd gotten

that close. Was it really possible he'd paid that much attention to her? As much as she had to him?

"You liked snow," he continued, his voice so low it was almost a whisper. "I watched you out the window once in Marketing and Management class. Everyone else ducked for cover and ran inside, but you lifted your head up and stayed out there after the bell, spinning around and catching flakes on your tongue. You looked like a snow fairy." He put a warm hand on her thigh and gave it a squeeze. "How am I doing?"

Her heart practically lurched out of her chest, but she covered it with a wobbly laugh. "Were you having me followed or something? Bugging my locker?"

"Nah." He nudged her with his shoulder, sending pinpricks of awareness racing down to her fingertips. "Just observant."

"Why me? Pretty much every girl in school had a crush on you. And a few of the guys, too."

"None of them were you. Especially the guys." He waggled his eyebrows but then turned serious, hesitating before he spoke next, almost as if he was weighing his words. "You're an amazing person, Holly. Then and now. When are you going to believe that?"

"Probably about the same time I believe in unicorns, the Easter Bunny and world peace."

"I'd sure like to try to convince you." He leaned into her, stroking a work-roughened finger down her arm. "That you're pretty damn incredible, I mean. I'm on the fence about unicorns, myself."

"Don't. Please." She scooted away from him. "I'm not who you think I am."

"Why don't you let me be the judge of that?"

Why didn't she? Because she was afraid of what his verdict would be, that was why. He'd never look at her the same way once he found out what she'd done. Or, more accurately, didn't do. Although she hated to admit it, she kind of liked the way he'd been looking at her. The way he was looking at her now.

"Have you ever had a secret so big you felt as if it could swallow you whole?" Holly's voice sounded breathy and faint, even to her ears. "One you kept from almost everyone?"

"Yeah, I have." He scrubbed a hand through his hair. "Tell you what. I'll share mine if you share yours."

"Okay." She paused and took a deep, fortifying breath. "You asked what made me leave Clark. I'll tell you, but you have to promise you won't hate me."

"I could never hate you." His voice was earnest, his eyes sincere.

She hoped he was right.

"You might when you hear this." He started to interrupt, but she stopped him with a shake of her head. She gazed back out at the lake, afraid if she looked at him the words wouldn't come. "I didn't leave because I was brave. Or smart. Or even just plain fed up, although I was. I left because I had to. I left because I was pregnant."

"I WAS PREGNANT," she repeated, as if trying to convince herself it was true. She hugged her knees to her chest. "That's why I got out. Or tried to. I didn't want my child to suffer what I'd gone through. The constant put-downs. Living on pins and needles, never knowing what was going to set Clark off. He'd rant and rave and throw things. Shoes, plates, my grandmother's antique porcelain doll. Once he even punched a hole in the living room wall. He was never physical with me," she added quickly. "Not until…that day. He came home early and found me packing…."

Her voice trailed off and she didn't have to say any

more for Nick to understand. The scars. The way her eyes had clouded over when he'd asked her if she had any children. It all made sense now. Horrible, awful, stomach-churning sense.

And she didn't think she was brave? "I don't know what to say."

"You don't have to say anything." Holly turned and her bottle-green eyes met his, causing his chest to constrict in a way that was becoming all too familiar. "Just listening helps."

"I could always take him out for you," he offered, only half joking.

"Thanks, but no, thanks. Clark's where he belongs. At the Charles E. Walker Correctional Center. And he's not up for parole for another seven years."

"Parole?" Nick practically choked on the word. "He's a goddamn murderer. He should be locked up for the rest of his natural life."

She shook her head. "I was still in my first trimester, not far enough along for them to charge him with murder. He got ten years for first-degree assault."

Nowhere near long enough, if you asked Nick. But he let the matter drop, knowing if he kept this line of questioning up he'd lose the shaky grip he had on his temper and probably scare her.

"I wish I could have been there for you," he said, surprised to find he really meant it. For the first time in his life, he wanted to do more for a woman than give her brief sexual pleasure. He wasn't sure why—and he wasn't sure he wanted to figure it out—but something about Holly brought his protective instincts to the surface.

"You're here now." She brushed a stray hair off her cheek and his temper faded, replaced by the growing urge to wrap her in his arms and keep her there, safe from scum-bags like Clark.

"I sure am."

With a puff of breath that ruffled her bangs across her forehead, she released her knees and let her legs swing off the end of the dock.

"I feel— I don't know. Lighter, somehow."

"You've never told anyone about this?"

"Only the police. The doctors and nurses who treated me. And my therapist. Clark pleaded guilty, so I didn't have to testify. The prosecutor said I wouldn't have been allowed to tell the jury about the baby, anyway. Said it wasn't 'relevant.'" She stared up at the sky, its brilliant blue now streaked with reds and yellows as the sun started to dip toward the horizon.

Not relevant, my ass. Nick mentally added another person to his list of people who deserved a good old-fashioned beat-down. "What about your family?"

"They had no idea how bad things were until I wound up in the hospital. And they still don't know about the baby. I could never bring myself to tell them."

"Why now?" His voice was halting as he lowered himself down to lie on the dock beside her. "Why me?"

She lifted one shoulder and let it fall. "You asked. And I guess I figured if anyone would understand, it'd be you."

She had a point there. "Thanks." He held his hand out again and this time she took it, entwining her fingers with his.

"For what?"

"For trusting me."

They lay like that, on their backs, hands joined, eyes on the reddening sky, the only sounds the lapping of the water against the dock, the chirping of crickets and an occasional birdcall. After a few minutes, she broke their silence.

"He wasn't always a jerk, you know. Things were great for the first few years. But then he lost his tenure-track position at Wesleyan and had to take a job at a small college in upstate Vermont. He was never really the same after that."

"You don't have to make excuses for him."

"I'm not. I'm making excuses for me."

"You don't have to do that, either."

"I killed my baby, Nick."

Her words were less than a whisper. He turned his head to look at her and found her gazing back at him, her eyes dark and wet and sad. "No. Clark did that."

"If I had left sooner, convinced him to take anger management classes, gone to my parents for help..."

"We can play what-if all day, but there's no guarantee any of that would have changed anything. You tried to protect your child. It's more than a lot of people do." More than his mother had done. He'd accepted her limitations a long time ago, understood that she loved him the best she could. But she loved her husband more. She didn't see how the man terrorized his son, convinced herself it was just discipline.

Who was making excuses now?

He sat up, rolling his eyes at his own stupidity. Definitely time for a change of subject. For both their sakes.

"My turn." Still holding her hand, he pulled her up beside him. "Although, to be honest, my secret seems sort of insignificant now."

"It was important enough for you to keep. That makes it significant."

Damn. How did she do that? Cut right through all his crap and leave him wide-open.

"I can't read."

She stared at him, a half smile on her face as if she

thought he was joking. "But you're an actor. You read scripts all the time. I've watched you do it for hours at rehearsal."

"Garrett records stuff for me so I can listen to it on my iPod. You know how you hassled me for always keeping one earbud in? That's how I follow along."

"I don't understand. You graduated from high school. Didn't you go to Juilliard? What did you do then?"

"My mom helped me with homework in high school. I had a tutor in college, and use a lot of audiobooks. Julliard lets dyslexic students take tests in the study center. Reading will always be a struggle for me, but I've learned how to deal with it."

She tilted her head, studying him. "Yet you chose a career that forces you to read. A lot."

"It's worth it if you love it. And I do." He squeezed her hand. "You helped me see that."

"What you've accomplished is pretty incredible. Why don't you talk about it more?"

"I will. Someday. But I want to be known as a serious actor first, not the actor with a learning disability."

"Who else knows?"

"Garrett, obviously. My assistant. And now you."

The quiet between them descended again and they lay back down on the dock. He absently stroked the back of her hand with his thumb, and was rewarded with a slight shiver.

"Nick?" She ran her tongue across her lips, which got things stirring south of the border.

"Yeah?"

She surprised him by rolling to her side, propping herself up on her elbow and throwing one leg over his hip, dangerously close to the south-of-the-border action. "Kiss me."

He tried his hardest to look apprehensive. If she wanted to play the seducer, he was on board 100 percent. "Out here?"

She arched a brow and deepened her voice, imitating him earlier. "I can't think of anyplace better. Can you?"

"No." He raised himself up to meet her gaze, reaching over with his free hand to cup her cheek. His lips were mere inches from hers, so close he could almost taste that raspberry lip gloss she liked so much. "I sure as hell can't."

16

HOLLY CLOSED HER eyes, sighing, as Nick's mouth met hers. He took his time, kissing her softly before teasing her lips with his tongue. She opened and breathed him in, letting his tongue caress hers. His hand drifted down to her hip, pulling her tight against him.

Sliding his hand to her shoulder, he inched down the strap of her sundress, and she tensed. He raised his head and drew back.

"Where we go from here's up to you, sweetheart." The challenge was apparent in his eyes. "But my vote's for whatever gets us naked fastest."

"That's the part that worries me."

"Afraid someone will see us?"

She nodded, fingering his shirt, loving the feel of the massive chest and ripped abs underneath.

He lifted her chin with his finger and she saw the laughter all over his face. "Isn't that part of the thrill?"

"Yes, but I'd rather not get caught in the buff."

"How about another compromise, like with the lights?" He slid the strap back onto her shoulder, pressing a kiss where it rested. "We do this with our clothes on."

"That sounds…complicated."

"I'm game." He rolled onto his back, pulling her on top of him. "Are you?"

"I've never been one to back down from a dare." She straddled him, feeling the growing bulge under his shorts.

"Good." He sat up and gripped her hips, raising her off him. "Spread your dress to cover us and unzip me."

She fluffed out her skirt and reached underneath, popping the button on his shorts and sliding down the zipper. After a few moments of embarrassed fumbling, she managed to free him from his boxers. He sprang forward, hot, hard and ready, in her palm.

"Please tell me you've got a thong on under there," he moaned against her neck, his lips leaving a wet line on her heated skin. "Or better yet, nothing at all."

"We were with a bunch of high schoolers. Of course I'm wearing underwear." She moved the crotch of her panties to one side and positioned the tip of his penis, wet with pre-cum, at her entrance. "Tiny, lacy, pink underwear." *Thank you, Noelle.* "I'm sure if you try hard enough you can work around them."

He raised his head and gave her that rakish bad-boy grin of his that always made her toes curl. "I live to try hard."

She started to lower herself onto him, but the hands at her waist tightened, stopping her. "Condom," he groaned, feeling around to his back pocket. "Shit."

"What's wrong?"

"I left my wallet in the glove compartment."

She swiveled her head toward the driveway, the car a distant speck across the lawn. "I'm on the pill," she panted, desperate to take him into her body with or without barrier. "And I'm clean. I was tested after Clark… You know. And I haven't slept with anyone since." Heat crept up her cheeks. "Except you."

"Same here. The insurance company made me get tested before rehearsals started."

"Remind me to thank them."

On a groan, she sank down, taking him inside her. His length filled her, stretching her, stroking her. Their mouths came together in full, wet contact, his probing tongue mirroring the slow, seductive back-and-forth of his penis. He tasted of peppermint and something else, something she couldn't identify, something elementally Nick.

He anchored one arm around her waist, using the other to brace himself on the dock, and thrust upward, hitting at just the right angle to send her spiraling out of control. Sweat beaded on his forehead and on the rippling muscles of his arms. She arched her head to lick one salty drop from his neck, nipping the tender flesh as she did.

"I'm not going to last long if you keep that up," he rasped. "God, Holly, what you do to me…"

She tried to talk but could barely breathe so she wrapped her arms around him, clinging to his shoulders. Her hands traveled up through his hair then down his back, slipping under his shirt and luxuriating in the feel of his muscles rippling with effort beneath his skin.

The wood rubbed against her knees and her head tilted back, hair ruffling in the breeze. She shifted to put more pressure on the spot that felt so, so good.

Oh, yeah. There. Right there.

"Come for me, sweetheart." His low, commanding growl turned her nipples into hard points that scraped against the lace of her bra. "Touch yourself while I fuck you."

He took one of her hands and brought it under her dress between them so their fingers brushed through her pubic hair and down to wet skin. She never did this—*never*—but he moved his hand over hers in a rough back-and-forth, pressing hard. It felt like a second heartbeat down there, pulsing with a rhythm she controlled. When he pulled his hand away she kept going, moving from her fingers to her palm and changing the pressure. Crazy, crazy lust pounded through her, strange noises coming from her throat that she'd never heard before, until she burst wide open, tiny dots dancing before her eyes.

"Do you have any idea how sexy you look when you come? Head back. Eyes half-closed. Your cheeks are flushed and those luscious lips are parted just enough so I can see the tip of that naughty little tongue. And the moans and whimpers you make…" He kissed her again, fast and intense, as he continued to move inside her. "You wreck me, babe."

She wrecked him? The only thing she'd ever wrecked was her brother's ten-speed, and she felt the same now as she had then, right before she crashed. Uninhibited. Out of control. She wanted to slow down, but Nick's thrusts bucked her back into motion and she rode him faster as the tension began to build again, low in her belly. Like a woman possessed, she clutched at his shoulders with her free hand, her nails digging into his skin.

"I'm close." He pressed his fingers into the soft, wet folds of her vagina, finding the sensitive button there. "Let go with me."

She shuddered and cried out again.

"That's it, baby." He ground out the words, watching her through half-lowered lids. A muscle in his jaw jumped in time with his continued thrusts. "I wish you could see yourself. Next time we have to find a mirror."

Holly moaned at that image, watching them make love in the mirror on her closet door, wild and mindless, rocking naked against each other. "You'd like that, wouldn't you?" He ducked his head to nuzzle her cheek. When he reached her ear, his tongue stole out to tease the lobe.

"Mmm." The cross between a moan and a hum was all she could manage, with her lips and tongue still unable to function. Her head dropped back and she dipped her fingers lower, brushing against his erection, like velvet over steel as he pumped in and out, her movements teasing him as much as herself.

She continued to stroke herself as they moved together, her soft flesh against his hard, until her inner muscles tightened around him and she spiraled into a climax so powerful it shook her, spun her and wrung her dry. Nick followed, stifling his cry by sinking his teeth into her shoulder, sending another mini-orgasm, like an aftershock, through her body.

They clung to each other as the tremors subsided, forehead to forehead, sweat-slickened and panting. Nick was first to recover, giving Holly a soft, slow kiss. "You okay?"

"I can't move."

"You don't have to. I've got you. I won't let anything happen to you."

"I know."

"I mean it." He cupped her chin. "Nothing bad happens to you on my watch."

She nodded and shifted to lay her head on his chest. "You sound like a superhero."

"Almost." He wrapped his arms around her. "They wanted me for one of the Marvel pictures. But I had to back out before the final screen test. I was under contract on a competing project that never got made. Then Trent Savage came along, and the rest is history."

"You lead an interesting life."

"It has its moments. But can be a pain in the ass. Trust me."

They sat quietly as the sky darkened and stars began to appear.

Holly shivered in the cooling night air and snuggled

closer to his chest. The steady, reassuring beat of his heart reverberated through her. "We should go soon."

"Are you cold?"

"A little."

He held her tighter, resting his chin on her head. "One more minute."

She sighed, burying her face in his neck, loving his smell and how the scruff of his beard tickled her cheek. "I like it here."

"Me, too. Always did."

"I liked— You know." Blushing, she looked down to her lap where their bodies were still joined under her dress.

He pulled back and tipped his head to look at her, hitting her again with that bad-boy grin. "You dirty girl. Was this your first trip to the wild side?"

"You could say that." She licked her lips and smiled. "But not my last, I hope."

"Not if I can help it." He lifted her up, separating them. "Come on, let's get you home."

"Okay." She kissed his neck. "But first I want…"

He moved his mouth to hers, but she turned her head so his lips brushed her cheek.

"…ice cream."

NICK YAWNED AND stretched as the morning sun slanted through the blinds on the window next to his bed, shooting warm rays across his bare chest.

Morning sun? Shit.

He shot out of bed, throwing off the sheet covering his legs. He should have been up hours ago. Holly's parents were spending the day at some home-and-garden show, and he'd promised to help her patch the greenhouse roof.

Not that he was surprised he'd overslept. The past three days had him damn near exhaustion.

And the past three nights.

Between helping out at the nursery in the mornings, PR crap in the afternoons and nights of marathon sex, he'd barely had time to breathe, much less sleep. The whens, wheres and hows of their nighttime activities had been... interesting. With their respective bedrooms just a few doors down from her parents', they'd resorted to getting it on in the strangest places. The greenhouse—during a thunderstorm, sweet-smelling and steamy. The toolshed—dark and musty, and the metal rake jabbing his ass was a major mood killer. The bed of her father's pickup truck—a little hard on his back, but not as bad as he expected once they put a blanket down.

On the one hand, it was a little ridiculous for two mature, consenting adults to be skulking around like guilty teenagers. On the other, it was exciting as hell. And the sex was nothing short of incredible. They'd spent the nights touching, tasting, learning each other's bodies. He discovered a spot behind her knee that made her melt. And she found out he was ticklish—but only on the bottoms of his feet.

Not once had they made it back to their own beds before 2:00 a.m. So, yeah, oversleeping wasn't a shock. What he couldn't figure out was why Holly hadn't woken him. Was she sacked out herself? The thought of her snug and sleep-rumpled, hair sticking up in odd directions, the imprint of her pillow on her cheek, had his chest doing that uncomfortable squeezing thing that was becoming, it seemed, an almost daily occurrence.

Ignoring the feeling—or trying to—he threw on a T-shirt and struggled into his jeans and work boots. After a quick check of his cell phone—texts from Garrett and a few of his buddies in L.A., nothing that couldn't wait—he headed downstairs, following the smell of fresh-brewed coffee to the kitchen. Still half-asleep, he almost missed the note taped to the cabinet above the coffeepot.

Nick,
We got the thumbs-up from the fire marshal, and I'm at the theater with Ethan. Figured you could use a morning in. Meet me there when you can.
Holly

He snuck a glance at the clock over the stove, which read a few minutes shy of noon. A quick cup of coffee and a shower and he could be over there before one. He filled a mug and headed upstairs.

Still in the shower half an hour later, hot water pounding his neck and back, he knew he was stalling. The show was back in business. Ethan was already in New Haven, the rest of the cast and crew sure to follow in a matter of days. He should be barrel-jumping for joy. So why wasn't he?

Reality was about to burst the lust-filled bubble he and Holly had been living in. That was why. And Nick wasn't sure how people would react to their being together. Hell, he wasn't even sure of his own reaction.

He shivered in the cooling water. Was he ready to call what they were doing a—*relax, big guy*—relationship? Take it public? Not in a smile-for-the-camera way, but for real?

He closed his eyes and let the water stream over him, picturing them together. Holding hands across the table at an intimate bistro. Sharing a smile across a crowded rehearsal room. Stealing a kiss backstage.

Yeah, he thought with a surprised smile. Call it corny, but for the first time in his life, he wanted all that. Her parents didn't know they were even dating—suspicions aside—and Nick wondered why the hell not. Sneaking around was getting old. He wanted to share a bed with her at night.

He wasn't made for marriage or forever. Those things had locked his mother in a life of misery and kept her from leaving a bad situation. Nick had vowed long ago not to get himself, or any woman, into that bind. And the demands of his career made even long-term unlikely. But he could give Holly all of himself, for as long as it lasted. And he didn't give a damn who knew about it.

Now the question was, did Holly?

He shut off the water and reached for a towel. Blotting the droplets from his face and hair, he stepped out of the shower and knotted the towel around his waist. With one hand on the sink, he used the other to wipe the steam off the mirror and stared at his reflection.

Holly had a lot more to lose if they came out of the closet, so to speak. She'd be the one left behind when he moved on to his next project, wherever in the world that took him. Was she willing to risk that?

There was only one way to find out. Nick scowled at himself in the mirror and reached for his razor. His beard could use a trim, and he wanted to look his best when he put his plan into action. He fought off a smile as he lathered up. What he was about to do made him feel as if he was seventeen again, anxious and overeager. Which was fitting, since it was what he'd wanted but was too chicken to do back in high school.

He was going to ask Holly to go steady with him.

17

"So what do you think?" Holly twirled around center stage, taking in the crown moldings, the gold filigree, the rich red of the heavy velvet house curtain. "Isn't it beautiful?"

She'd fallen in love with the Rep in all its majesty when she was twelve and her parents brought the family to a production of *Oklahoma!* Noelle had been all about the big ballet sequence in the second act. Ivy had wanted to know why she couldn't take pictures in the theater. Gabe had dissected the plot, pointing out every flaw. But Holly had sat in her plush cushioned seat, open-mouthed and stock-still, transfixed by it all—the music, the lights, the costumes, the sets—from the first downbeat to the last curtain call.

Even the audience members had fascinated her, in their varied and eclectic versions of theater dress-up. Now the Rep audience would see her words performed on that stage. Okay, so her Broadway dream had gone up in smoke. In some ways, being at the Rep was a lot more meaningful.

Why had it taken her so long to get back to the stage? She'd always felt at home there. Too bad she couldn't leap right from that starstruck kid lip-synching with Ado Annie to this moment. No string of failed jobs. No Clark. No miscarriage.

"Yeah." Nick's voice brought her back to the present. "Beautiful."

She stopped twirling to face him, hands on her hips. "You're not even looking."

"Oh, I'm looking, all right." He leaned against the stage-left proscenium arch, his eyes raking her up and down.

"At the theater, hot stuff." She stuck her tongue out at him, laughing. "I can't believe they used to keep highway equipment in here."

"They did?"

"This place started life as a vaudeville house. When that died out, the Department of Transportation used it for storage. The condition of the building got so bad the state wanted to tear it down until a group of preservationists bought it for a dollar. It took them four years to restore, but I think the result was worth it." She did another quick turn. "Don't you?"

"Don't I what?"

"Have you heard a word I've said?"

"Not really. I was too distracted by the whole Marilyn Monroe thing going on with your skirt." He made a circle with his finger. "Spin around again."

"You have a one-track mind."

"Name one guy who doesn't."

"Mr. Spock."

"He's a fictional character. And even he'd be tempted by you in that outfit." He gave her a scorching look that made her knees wobble. "Did you know I can see your nipples in that shirt?"

She looked down and pulled at her blouse. "Cannot."

"Can too. Are you sure you're wearing a bra?"

She couldn't help but laugh at his persistence. The sheer force of his will—and his charm—was overwhelming. "You're hopeless."

"More like hopeful." He crossed the stage and came up behind her. His hands settled on her waist, his mouth at her ear. "How much time do we have before lunch?"

"I don't know." She tilted her head back so he could kiss her neck. "Another half an hour or so. Ethan said he'd be done around two. Why?"

"Ever make out onstage?" He spun her in his arms so they were facing each other and lifted her off her feet. The start of his erection pressed against her belly.

"No," she said on a breathless laugh, her hands coming up to grip his shoulders. "But I'm sure you have."

"Only when it was scripted." He cupped her bottom, holding her tight. "This would be my first attempt at improvisation."

A noise in the wings made her freeze. "Did you hear that?"

"I thought we already established that my one-track mind's incapable of focusing on anything else when you're around." He lowered his mouth to hers, stopping a breath away from her parted lips.

"Wait." She drew her head back and cocked it to one side, listening. Nothing. She breathed a sigh of relief, but the close call had rattled her. "We can't do this. What if someone sees us?"

"You didn't seem to have a problem with that on the dock, as long as we kept our clothes on." His chocolate eyes danced with mischief. "And as much as I'd like to, I'm not planning on us stripping center stage."

She blushed at the memory of how she'd writhed all over him like a sexually frustrated python, not caring where they were or who might stumble across them. "This is different. We're going to be working in this theater. Living here, too. We'll be with these people day and night for the next six weeks."

He let her slide down the length of his body to the floor and she instantly regretted opening her big fat mouth.

"Would that bother you?" He loosened his hold but kept her in the circle of his arms. "Them finding out about us?"

"I don't know. I haven't really thought about it, but if they knew we were…together…it might get awkward."

"So you don't want to take this public?"

"I don't even know what 'this' is."

"You. Me. Together." He slipped a hand down to the small of her back and pressed her against his hardness. "Having hot monkey sex every chance we get."

"Like friends with benefits?" Holly shuddered. Was that what they were doing? It sounded so sordid when she put it that way. She would've said they were "seeing each other," but that sounded just as casual. Not the kind of thing she should be risking her reputation for. She'd earned this gig. Belonged here. She didn't want anyone to say she'd slept her way to success.

"What I feel for you is far from friendship, babe. I've never had a woman turn me inside out like you do. I like being with you. I want to keep being with you. Only you." He reached up to caress her cheek, brushing his wayward thumb across her lips. "But I won't lie to you, Holly. If you're looking for forever, I'm not your guy."

Ouch.

She'd known going in he was only hers on loan. He'd always have his work, his fans pulling him away. But she'd been okay with that, or so she thought.

So why did it hurt so much to hear him say it?

"Been there, done that." Her tone was purposefully bright, her game face firmly in place. "Forever's not all it's cracked up to be. I've learned to live for the here and now."

"Then we're good?" He bent his head, bringing his lips within striking distance again.

"Hold on, superstar." She slipped out of his arms and crossed down to the apron of the stage, out of range of his lethal sex appeal. "I get that we're…temporary. But that's all the more reason for us to be discreet."

He joined her in a few long strides. "So you want to keep sneaking around like horny teenagers?"

"You've got to admit, it has its advantages."

"You weren't the one with a rake stabbing you in the ass."

"And you won't be the one left behind when this temporary thing runs its course."

A flash of something that looked like remorse darkened Nick's eyes. "You're right," he said, taking her hand. "I'm in no position to make demands. If you want to keep things between us quiet, then quiet it is. I can be stealthy. Your own personal love ninja."

Her heart did a little flip-flop at the word *love,* but her head knew he didn't mean anything beyond its "making." She took in his broad shoulders, muscular chest and all-around imposing build and shook her head. "I can't quite picture you as a ninja. Of any kind. But I appreciate the offer."

"Are you questioning my ninja prowess?" he teased, weaving his fingers between hers. "Haven't you seen any of my movies? Trent Savage is an expert in karate, kendo and jujitsu, and has been known to dabble in the ancient Chinese art of yiquan, or mind boxing."

"Mind boxing?"

"Yeah, it's—"

"Never mind," she said, forcing a laugh. "I take it back. Forget I ever doubted you."

Reminder to self: be casual.

She could do it. She had to. The only other option was breaking up now and that was—well, not an option.

"Come on." He tugged on her hand, pulling her in the direction of the stage door. "All of a sudden I've lost my appetite. For food, that is. What do you say we head back to the homestead?"

"What about Ethan?"

"Text him. Tell him something more important came up."

"Oh, yeah?" She willed the corners of her mouth to curl up into what she hoped was a convincing smile, playing the part of lighthearted lover, even though another part of her was dying inside. That part wanted the white picket fence, two-point-five kids, a minivan in the driveway and a golden retriever in the backyard.

She knew she'd never have any of that with Nick. She also knew Nick might ruin her for any other man.

But oh, what a way to go.

Asking for more than a love affair with him was beyond greedy, and, flawed as she was, greed had never been one of Holly's vices. She stood on tiptoe and kissed his lips lightly. "Like what?"

"Like we've only got a few hours until your parents get back from the garden show, and I need to practice my stealth moves."

"You didn't have to come all the way up here to check on me." Holly emptied another packet of sweetener into her chai latte. "I'm fine."

"Oh, yes, I did." Devin took a sip of her dark French roast. Black. No girlie drinks for her. "And you're not fine. You should have heard yourself on the phone. You sounded like one of those heroines in a country song. You know, your husband left, your dog died and your pickup won't start."

"Since I don't have a husband, a dog or a pickup, I think

your friend-in-distress radar is out of whack." Holly stared out the coffee shop window at the theater across the street where the cast was still deep in rehearsal, opening night only a few days away. With the script finally set after two weeks of rewrites, Ethan had practically pushed her out the door when Devin showed up, making one of her spur-of-the-moment, hey-I-was-in-the-neighborhood-so-I-thought-I'd-pop-in visits.

Had he sensed the tension between her and Nick? They'd tried to keep things light and breezy, but Holly had to admit it was wearing on her, being with him and not being with him at the same time. On more than one occasion, she'd caught herself staring at him across the rehearsal room, or in the greenroom at lunchtime, unable to so much as touch him when only hours before they'd been naked and sweaty in each other's arms.

"Fine." Devin leaned back in her chair, crossing her long, model-thin legs, bare from the hem of her short skirt to the top of her thigh-high, black stiletto boots. No less than three men had stopped to stare at her, causing a near pile-up at the take-out counter. "Don't tell me what crawled up your ass and died. I'll worm it out of you eventually. In the meantime I can entertain you with stories of how I tormented your brother on the way up here."

Holly shook her head, smiling. "I still can't believe you convinced Gabe to give you a ride."

"What can I say?" Devin lifted one shoulder in a half-hearted shrug and reached for a cinnamon roll from a plate in the center of the table. "I'm very persuasive. When I want to be. I needed to see you. The chance to wrinkle his oxford was an extra incentive."

"My brother's a good guy. He's just…tightly wound."

"As a yo-yo." Devin licked crumbs from her ruby-red

lips, resulting in another near collision. "He needs a few lessons in loosening up. Maybe more than a few."

"Are you volunteering to teach him?"

"No way," Devin choked out, almost spitting coffee across the table. "We don't mix well. Like tequila and orange juice. He played classical music the entire two-hour trip. If I didn't have Hendrix on my iPod, I'd have jumped ship when he stopped for gas at the Fairfield rest area. But enough about me. Start talking."

Holly's head snapped forward and she straightened in her seat. "I thought that's what we were doing."

"I was talking. You were listening. Now it's your turn. What's bugging you?"

"I told you. I'm fine."

"That's bullshit and we both know it." Devin pulled her cell phone from the bag hanging off her chair and slid her finger across the screen. "Maybe I should call your mother. Get some insider info on what kind of trouble you could've gotten into up here in suburbia."

Great. Holly had been so busy with rewrites and rehearsals she hadn't seen much of her parents since she'd moved into company housing two weeks ago. She was lucky and didn't have to double up like some of the others. Her furnished apartment was small—even smaller than her place in New York—but it was private, a place for her and Nick to get together away from the watchful eyes of the cast and crew. And while she missed her mom's cooking, it was worth it not to have her butting into Holly's so-called love life.

"Okay, you win. Put the phone away." Holly took a sip of her latte, gathering her courage.

"I'm sleeping with Nick."

"Hallelujah!" Devin shouted so loudly a few of the patrons who'd been ogling her earlier turned to glare at her.

Not that that made her lower her voice one bit. "It's about freaking time you got some action. When did it start? The night you two were at the bar, right? I'll bet he's an animal in the sack."

"Keep it down, will you?" Holly hissed, smiling apologetically at the other diners before turning her attention back to Devin. "This isn't for public consumption."

"Why the hell not?" Devin asked only slightly more softly. "If I were screwing Nick Damone I'd be screaming it from the top of the Empire State Building."

"I'm sure you would. But we're different people. I don't want to flaunt it, for a lot of reasons. Mainly because, as sweet and hot and good as it is, it's going to be over soon enough. No additional speculation needed."

"Nice try. But you can't fool me, Holls. I know you." Devin leaned forward, resting her elbows on the table. "Don't try to pretend this isn't what's bothering you. Casual relationships are my style, not yours."

"Maybe I'm trying to change that. After all, the last serious relationship I had didn't turn out that well." Holly tilted her chin up defiantly. Why was it so hard for Devin to believe she was as modern and liberated as the next gal? If Nick wanted a no-strings-attached affair, that was fine by her.

Liar. Holly might just be the world's worst good-time girl, going by her behavior at the theater this week. Sure, she was the one who'd proposed their whole cloak-and-dagger bit. But she sucked, big-time, when it came to pulling it off, because of one simple, inescapable, immutable fact.

Despite all her determination, her precautions, her dire warnings to herself, she'd fallen in love with Nick Damone.

Devin raised a brow at Holly over her French roast. "A leopard can't change its spots."

The unmistakable nasal vibrato of Ethel Merman belting out "There's No Business Like Show Business" rang out from under the table, saving Holly from another lackluster attempt to convince her friend she was happy being Nick's current fling. She bent down and rummaged around in her purse, finally yanking out her cell phone. "That's Ethan. I'd better get it. He might need me back at the theater."

"Script emergency?" Devin smirked. "Or maybe he wants you to bring Malcolm a cinnamon roll."

"Hey, Ethan, we're just finishing up…." Holly felt the blood drain from her face as she listened to him. Her palms started to sweat and she almost dropped the phone. "Oh, my God, is he…?" Heart pounding, she slung her purse strap over her shoulder and stood, knocking her chair over in her rush for the door. "Okay. I'm on my way. I'll meet you at the hospital."

"Wait up." Devin was at her side in a flash, racing with her across the street to her VW. "What's wrong?"

"There's been an accident at the theater."

"Is it…?"

"Nick. He's hurt."

"What happened?"

"I'm not sure. Ethan said something about one of the lights falling." They reached the car and Holly fumbled for her keys, blinking back tears. She didn't want to let Devin see she was an emotional basket case, but the thought of Nick injured—or worse—tore at her like a knife to the gut.

Or to the heart.

"You're in love with him, aren't you?" Devin asked, her voice uncharacteristically gentle.

"I'm not… I can't be…" One look at her friend's face told Holly her denial fell on deaf ears. Admitting defeat, she slumped against the car and let her tears fall freely. "Oh, God, Dev. What if he…?"

"He's going to be all right. He has to be." Devin pried the keys from Holly's hand, opened the driver's door and motioned Holly around to the other side of the car. "Get in. I'm driving."

"You don't know where we're going," Holly protested even as her feet carried her to the passenger's door. Numb, she opened it and got in, swiping away tears with the back of her hand.

"So you'll give me directions. You're in no condition to drive." Devin slid in behind the wheel and started the engine. Before putting it in gear, she reached into her bag and handed Holly a pack of tissues and her cosmetics case. "Here. Dry your eyes and make yourself pretty. The last thing Nick or anyone else needs to see is you falling apart."

"Th-thanks." Holly pulled a mirror from the case, flipped it open and made a halfhearted stab at pulling herself together to pacify her friend.

"Don't mention it." Devin maneuvered out of the parking space and into traffic. "Now, point me toward the hospital and I'll have you there faster than you can say 'last call.'"

18

EVERYTHING HURT.

From the ends of his hair to the soles of his feet, Nick's entire body was one enormous ache.

And the too-soft pillow and too-hard mattress weren't helping, either. Where the hell was he? Not his Malibu beach house or his apartment at the Plaza, that was for damn sure. Even the dump the Rep had set him up in had a bed more comfortable than the one he lay in now.

Nick struggled to open his eyes, the lids strangely heavy and uncooperative. When he finally succeeded, he moaned and slammed them shut against the harsh fluorescent lighting.

"Nicky?"

Mom?

He opened his eyes again, even more slowly this time, letting them adjust to the bright light.

He was in a world of white. Walls, sheets, blanket, floor. A tube ran from his arm to an IV bag hanging on a metal stand, and a monitor clipped to his finger relayed his pulse to a machine beeping at regular intervals in the corner.

Shit. The beeps picked up speed as Nick went into panic mode. He was hurt, clearly. Badly enough to be flat on his back in a hospital bed, complete with tubes and wires. But how? The last thing he remembered, he was onstage, rehearsing a scene with Marisa. After that, his Swiss-cheese mind came up blank.

A ragged sob came from his bedside, and a bony hand, surprisingly strong, gripped his. "You're awake. Thank God." His mother's familiar voice washed over him and the beeping from the pulse monitor slowed. "I'll go get the nurse."

She started to rise, but Nick held her hand as if it were a lifeline.

"Stay," he croaked, his mouth so dry ribbons of pain shot down his throat. He turned his head to look at her—more pain—and spied a plastic pitcher and cup on a rolling tray. "Water."

Nodding, she poured and lifted the cup. "Not too much," she warned. "Go slow."

He took a sip then sank back against the pillow. "Better. What happened?"

"The police said one of the lights came down. You were lucky. It missed your head and caught you on the shoulder. But you lost consciousness when you fell."

He didn't feel lucky. More like cursed. Maybe Marisa had a point.

Marisa. She'd been standing right next to him. Nick tried to sit up. "Marisa. Is she…?"

"She's fine." His mother brushed a lock of hair off his forehead and held out the cup for him to take another sip. "You pushed her out of harm's way."

"Good." With a relieved sigh, he closed his eyes. After a few minutes, he felt strong enough to open them again and brave the fluorescent glare. "How did you know I was hurt?"

"Your girlfriend called me."

"Holly?"

"She's lovely, Nicky. And she obviously cares for you a great deal."

That was both exactly what he wanted to hear and what he didn't. The more she cared about him, the harder it was going to be for him to leave her when the time came. "Where...?"

"She went to get me some coffee."

Damn, his mom was good. They spent most of their lives three thousand miles apart, and she could still finish his sentences for him.

"Dad?" he ventured, for some perverse reason needing her to voice what he already knew.

She shook her head. "I'm sorry, Nicky. I tried. You know how stubborn he is. He calls it 'tough love.'"

"He's got the 'tough' part down. 'Love'? Not so much."

"He's a fool." A rogue tear rolled down her cheek and she swiped it away.

"It's okay, Mom." He gave her hand a reassuring squeeze. "You're here. I'm surprised he agreed to that."

"He didn't." More tears, which his mother wiped with a tissue she pulled from her sweater. She had a pile going on the bedside table. "But I told him I had to come. That you're our son, whether he liked it or not."

Nick rubbed his forehead, convinced he'd entered the twilight zone. Either that or the light had hit him harder than anyone realized. Because he could have sworn his mother said she'd stood up for him against his father for the first time in, well, ever. "I'm sure that went over big."

She lifted her free hand, palm up, in an "oh, well" gesture. "He'll learn to deal with it if he wants his shirts pressed and dinner on the table at six."

"Seriously, Ma." Gritting his teeth, Nick managed to pull himself up a few inches, which his mother took as an invitation to force-feed him some more water. "He must be pissed as hell. He's probably trashing the place as we speak. You can't go back there."

"Your father's better now about throwing things. But he's still unforgiving about dinnertime. And only light starch on his shirts."

Nick groaned. "For God's sake, Ma. You're his wife, not a servant. I'm hiring a housekeeper and a cook. Hopefully, they can keep each other sane working for Dad. And you'd have time to do something for yourself for a change."

She shook her head. "I wouldn't know where to begin."

"What about the community garden? You used to love it there."

"Yes, I did." Her gaze became unfocused and her smile seemed faraway. "There's nothing quite like a row of sunflowers standing guard over ripe vegetables."

Her voice drifted off and he sat in silence, watching her daydream about gardens past.

Was she losing it? She seemed so much smaller—and not just physically—than she had when he was growing up. In their weekly phone calls, she always steered the conversation to him, as if she had nothing to say about her own life. Probably because she didn't have much of one. His father had cut her off from everything—and everyone—she loved.

"So go back. You belong there. I'm sure they'd be thrilled to have you."

"But how would I explain it to your father?"

He sighed. "Refuse to use the staff if you want, but I'm paying for them either way."

"Nicky!" His mother adjusted his blanket so it came up under his chin, making him feel a little like one of the mummies at the Museum of Natural History. "Such a waste. You wouldn't dare."

"Look at me, Ma." He shook off the blanket. "I'm

not kidding." Why hadn't he thought of this sooner? He couldn't believe after so much time it was this easy. The sliver of a person left in his mother's shell needed some time away from his father and out of that house of depression and angst.

"Well, then." She made a little humming sound, like her planning gears were kicking into motion. "I wouldn't want your money to go to waste. You work so hard. I'll tell your father they're my birthday gift. Would that be okay?"

Thank God. "That's fine, Ma. Whatever works."

She stood and leaned over the bed rail to give him a gentle hug. "Promise me you'll take better care of yourself, too. You work too hard. Enjoy yourself a little more. Maybe take that nice girl of yours on vacation."

"How about I take my two best girls on vacation when the show closes?" Nick asked when she reluctantly released him. By then he'd convince Holly to come clean about their relationship, at least to their friends and families. "The south of France sound good? Brad and Angelina offered to let me use their château in Brignoles."

"Brangelina?" She sucked in a breath and flushed, yet another victim of celebrity fever.

"Still reading the gossip rags, I see." He chuckled.

She ignored the dig, still lost in a starstruck trance. "I don't know, Nicky. I wouldn't want to impose."

Nick's headache faded, and a weight lifted off his chest. "You won't, Ma. Honest. They've got, like, thirty bedrooms. And a moat. I'll have my travel agent get you a passport and ticket."

"What will I tell your father?" He started to say he'd take care of the old man, but she cut him off with a wave of her hand. "Never mind. I know." She bounced on her toes like a giddy schoolgirl. "I'll tell him it's my Christmas present."

* * *

HE WAS AWAKE. Holly paused with her hand on the doorknob and listened, letting her heart flutter through its celebratory happy dance. The doctors said he'd be fine, but
this was better. This was proof.

She could hear Nick's voice alternating with his mom's,
both thick with emotion. She waited, not wanting to interrupt what was obviously a sensitive moment. When Nick
dropped Brad's and Angelina's names, she figured the
moment had passed and the coast was clear. With a not-
so-subtle cough to announce her presence, she pushed the
door open and went in.

"Here's your coffee." She handed the disposable cup to
Nick's mother and planted a kiss on the side of his face.
"You scared us to death."

He looked pale and haggard. She took a deep breath to
avoid the onset of another crying jag.

"I'm sure you two could use a few minutes to your-
selves." Nick's mother rose and crossed to the door. "I'm
going to call your father. He might not admit it, but he'll
want to know you're all right."

The *whoosh* of the door echoed in her wake.

Holly fiddled with a thread on her shirtsleeve, not sure
where to begin now that they were alone. She looked
around the cold, antiseptic room and shivered, the per-
vasive smell of disinfectant, mixed with sickness, making her stomach churn. Memories of her last hospital visit
overwhelmed her.

The pain.

The loneliness.

The loss.

"You okay?" Nick's voice, warm and gentle, snapped
her out of her trance.

"Shouldn't I be asking you that?"

"I'll be fine. Just tired."

"They're probably going to want to keep you overnight for observation. You were woozy for a while there."

"I think in this case I can live with one night." He managed a suggestive eyebrow waggle and she flushed, remembering the one-night, no-strings ultimatum she'd given him in New York. She'd been way off base that time. Hopefully, today's prediction was more accurate.

A flash of pain crossed Nick's face and he grimaced, closing his eyes and letting his head fall back into the pillow. Her heart lurched and she ached to crawl into the tiny bed with him, press herself against his back and soothe him with her entire body.

Not good.

It was time for some damage control. She took a long, deep breath and silently chanted what had become her inner mantra: *be casual.*

In a month, the show would be over and he'd move on to his next project. His next girl. All she had to do was use that time to wean herself off him, like a smoker on the nicotine patch. Except there wasn't a patch or gum to help her get over Nick. She'd have to do that all by herself.

His life was so different from hers. Brad and Angelina. European castles. Red-carpet premieres. Pretending she'd fit in was like acting out a play in her bedroom. Pure fantasy.

"I should go. You need to rest. Plus, the gang in the waiting room's probably desperate for news. Someone's got to stop them from storming the nurses' station."

He cracked one eye open. "Don't you want to wait for the doctor?"

"Your mom's got that covered. And I'll be back soon for a full report." She stood and started to release his hand, but he managed to hang on and pull her toward the bed.

"Can I get a goodbye kiss?" Both eyes open now, he mustered a smile, still devastating, even at half strength.

I love you.

Words she'd never hear from him.

And never say.

"Sure you're up for it?"

"Just a small one." He tapped his cheek with one finger. "Right here. To speed my recovery."

"Well, if it's for your health…" She bent down, lightly bussed his cheek, then scurried back a safe distance.

The man was her kryptonite, and she needed to survive their contact. Distance was essential.

"I feel better already." With a low moan that contradicted his words, he closed his eyes again and relaxed his grip on her hand.

Holly slipped from his grasp and out the door. Her footsteps quickened as she made her way down the hall to the waiting area, where a mob of anxious cast and crew members—and media and fans, if news of Nick's accident had leaked out—would swarm her for information the second she came through the security door.

She rounded the corner and braced herself for the explosion. No matter what was on the other side of that door, one thing was sure. She'd be safer with the crowd out there than in that suffocatingly small hospital room, alone with Nick.

19

"CAN I GET you some coffee, Mr. Damone? Or maybe a water?"

Nick was about to snap. He could get his own damn drink if he was thirsty. All the tests were negative and the doctor said he was ready for anything, but the way everyone at the theater was babying him, you'd think he was Tiny freaking Tim.

Then he saw the fresh-faced PA's earnest expression, and his words died in his throat. It wasn't this guy's fault Nick was in a pissy mood. What was his name? Les? No, Wes. He seemed like a decent guy, always the first one to jump up and offer assistance. Nick had seen him doing everything from ironing costumes to hanging lights.

"Thanks, Wes. Water would be great."

"Sure thing, Mr. Damone." Wes ran off in the direction of the greenroom.

"And you don't have to rush," Nick called to the PA's back. "It's not like I'm going to have you fired if you're not back in ten."

Like some people.

He stretched his legs and turned his attention back to his script. He had twenty minutes before rehearsal started, and with opening night less than two days away he needed every one of them to review Ethan's eleventh-hour blocking changes.

Cast and crew trickled in, greeting Nick and asking how he was feeling. Marisa gave him her cell number and told him to call her anytime—day or night—if he needed anything, and even Malcolm offered to bring him dinner and run lines together. He answered them politely but noncommittally, crumpling up Marisa's number and stuffing it in his pants pocket, then went back to work, burying his head in his script until the one person he wanted to see showed up.

Holly.

She'd stayed with him last night, waking him every couple of hours to make sure he was okay. But she hadn't slept with him. Not in the biblical or the literal sense. She'd insisted on taking the pullout in what passed for a living room, saying he needed a good night's sleep. Alone. And this morning, she'd left as soon as he was awake, claiming she had to meet with Ethan and the Aaronsons before rehearsal.

"Here's your water, Mr. Damone." Wes appeared at Nick's side, handed him a bottle and scurried away before Nick could even thank him.

"Okay, everyone." Ethan stood center stage, flanked by Holly's firefighter friend, Cade, and a police officer. The Aaronsons hung back, stage left, but there was no sign of Holly. "Take a seat."

"What's with the cop?" Malcolm asked, sliding into the seat next to Nick.

"Looks like we're about to find out."

"As you can see, some members of local law enforcement are here today and they're going to be with us for the rest of our run." Ethan held up a hand to stem the uproar that arose at his announcement. "Be patient, and Sergeant Chang will explain everything."

Ethan gestured to the police officer, who stepped forward. "The accident that injured Mr. Damone is under investigation. Until we determine the cause, Lieutenant Hardesty from the fire marshal's office and I will be checking IDs at the stage door and patrolling the backstage area. During performances, we'll have extra security in the house, as well."

"So you think someone was trying to hurt Nick?" one of the stagehands asked from the back row.

"We haven't ruled anything out," Cade stepped in to answer. "But with the fire, and the other suspicious incidents in New York, anything's possible."

Jesus Christ.

An audible hum spread throughout the theater, and Nick gripped the water bottle so tight the plastic crackled in his fist. Even after the arson, he hadn't wanted to believe someone was targeting them. Fires happened every day. So did power outages and food poisoning. He'd been too muddled in the hospital to put the pieces together, but now that his brain was semifunctional again, his near miss was too much for him to write off as coincidence.

"We're doing everything we can to ensure your safety," Ethan said, taking center stage again. "But we understand some of you may be uncomfortable continuing with the production. If so, please come talk to me, Ted or Judith privately, and we'll make arrangements for you to leave, no questions asked." He pushed back his shirtsleeve and checked his watch. "We'll start rehearsal in fifteen. Be back here and ready to go. We've got less than forty-eight hours until curtain and a hell of a lot of work to do."

"Holy shit," Malcolm muttered as Ethan and company left the stage. "This is serious."

"Want to bail?" Nick asked.

"Nah. If I avoided everyone who wanted to kill me, I'd never leave my apartment. You?"

"No way." As long as Holly was there, so was he. Nick took a sip of water and grimaced. "You were right. This stuff does taste like crap."

"Not really." Malcolm shoved his hands in his pockets and looked at his lap. "Just keeping the minions on their toes."

"Seriously, though." Nick held out the bottle. "Try it."

Malcolm hesitated, his eyes narrowing. "Where did you get that from?"

"One of the PAs. Wes."

"Short kid? Shaved head? Always wears a sweater vest?"

"That's him."

Malcolm whipped out a tissue and used it to grab the neck of the bottle.

"What the hell are you doing?"

"Preserving the evidence." Malcolm held the bottle away from his body. "I saw it when I did a guest-star role on *NCIS*."

"What evidence?"

"I might be paranoid," Malcolm said, dropping his voice to a whisper, "but I think our friend Wes tried to poison you."

"You wanted to see me, Mr. Phelps?" Wes's eyes darted from Ethan, to Nick, to Malcolm, then back to Ethan again.

"Sit down, Wes." Ethan motioned toward the empty chair across from the desk in his third-floor office.

"Is something wrong?" Wes shuffled to the chair and lowered himself into it.

"That depends." Nick leaned against the wall, arms crossed in front of his chest.

Wes swallowed visibly and plucked at the collar of his vest. "On what?"

"On what Sergeant Chang finds in the trash can in the greenroom." Ethan stood and walked around to the front of the desk.

"What does that have to do with me?"

"Tell him, Malcolm." Ethan sat on the corner of the desk, his eyes never leaving Wes.

"I saw you put something in Nick's water bottle."

"I… It's… That was mine. I'm fighting a cold. Jimmie Lee gave me some of that powdered vitamin C stuff everyone swears by."

"Nice try." Malcolm came from behind Wes to sit on the opposite corner of the desk. "But Nick said his water tasted funny. And you gave it to him."

"I did, but—"

The door swung open and Sergeant Chang entered, followed by Cade and Holly. Nick caught her eye for a brief second before she hid behind her friend.

"We found it." The police officer held up a clear plastic evidence bag with a small white bottle inside. "Eye drops. Ingested they can cause blurred vision, nausea, vomiting, seizures and even death."

Wes made a little choking sound. "Death? He told me…"

"He who?" Nick pushed off the wall.

"Before you say anything more I should advise you that you're under arrest." Sergeant Chang pulled Wes up by the shoulders, yanked his arms behind his back and handcuffed him. "You have the right to remain silent. Anything you say can and will be held against you in a court of law. You have the right to an attorney."

"What's going on here?" Ted squeezed into the already crowded office, trailed by his wife. "Why wasn't I called?"

"I was just about to," Ethan explained. "Wes spiked Nick's water bottle with prescription eye drops, and I'm pretty sure we'll find he's responsible for the fire and the other incidents, too. We didn't want to tip him off before we had him in custody."

"He's the one who should be in custody." With his hands cuffed behind his back, Wes could only jerk his head in Ted's direction.

"Get him out of here," Ted barked.

"Hold on." Cade stood in the doorway, his frame, though not as big as Nick's, more than large enough to block anyone from leaving. Nick tensed, ready to jump in if things got any uglier. "I'd like to hear what he has to say."

"I…I didn't want to hurt anyone." Wes's gaze ping-ponged from face to face, finally settling on Nick. "Honest. Mr. Aaronson swore he just wanted to scare everyone so the show would close."

"That's ridiculous," Ted huffed. "What reason would I have to shut down my own show?"

"I can think of a few million reasons." Judith, silent until now, stepped forward, distancing herself from her husband. "I'm filing for divorce. If this show fails, the value of our production company takes a huge hit, which would let Ted lowball me when he buys me out." She swiveled her head to look at him, her eyes brimming with confusion and regret. "Is that it, Ted? Do you hate me so much you'd rather lose a fortune than see me with it?"

"I built that company up from nothing," Ted snarled. "It's mine."

Holly shrank back from Ted and Nick reached for her, drawing her back against his chest and wrapping his arms around her to keep her there.

Where she belonged. Forever.

Nick pushed that unsettling thought aside and tried to focus on the scene playing out in front of him instead of the warm, soft, sweet-smelling woman in his arms. Cade had Ted in cuffs, and Sergeant Chang, with Wes still in hand, was reading the producer his rights.

"Do you understand these rights as they have been read to you?"

Ted muttered something Nick couldn't catch, but the police officer, apparently satisfied, nodded and addressed the group. "We're going to take these two down to the station for booking. We'll need to get statements from all of you in the next few days, so make sure we have your contact information."

"That's easy." Judith might have been responding to Sergeant Chang but her eyes were glued on her husband. "We'll be here, at the theater. We open Friday."

"Fat chance," Ted sneered, prompting Cade to tug on his cuffed wrists. "You can't pull it off alone."

"Watch me," she replied calmly, hands on her hips in a classic don't-fuck-with-me pose.

Nick fought off a smile. The lady had balls, keeping it together and facing off with her soon-to-be ex. She reminded him of Holly, going toe to toe with his father in the high school parking lot.

The next few minutes were a blur of activity. Cade and Sergeant Chang led Ted and Wes away. Judith and Ethan went in search of Jimmie Lee so they could work out what to tell the rest of the cast and crew and readjust the rehearsal schedule to make up for lost time. Malcolm took off, muttering something about having his assistants check his props and costumes for evidence of tampering.

"I should probably call my parents," Holly said, slipping out of Nick's arms and fleeing for the door the minute they were alone. "I don't want them to hear this through the Stockton grapevine."

"Wait." He caught her elbow. "Talk to me."

"About what?"

"About whatever's bothering you."

She gave him a smile that didn't quite reach her eyes. "You mean besides the fact that someone tried to kill my boyfriend and sabotage my play?"

He slid his hand from her elbow to her wrist, winding his fingers through hers. "I get the feeling there's something more than that. You've been acting funny ever since my trip to the hospital. Have I done something to upset you?"

"What could you have done?" She squeezed his hand. "You were practically comatose, remember?"

He frowned. "You're sure?"

"Sure, I'm sure." She went up on tiptoe to give him a quick, hard kiss. "We'll talk tonight. I promise."

Nick watched her go, a cold, dull ache growing in the pit of his stomach. Her words were right, but her behavior was all wrong, and he had the sinking feeling he'd just witnessed the beginning of their end.

20

THE BALLROOM OF the Omni Hotel glittered with refracted light from the crystal chandeliers. Smartly dressed waiters passed among the two hundred or so guests at the play's closing-night festivities, balancing trays laden with exotic hors d'oeuvres and flutes of champagne. The soft strains of a Gershwin tune underscored the buzz of conversation.

Taking advantage of a rare moment alone, Holly snagged a glass from a passing waiter and retreated to the far corner of the room. She found an empty table and sat down as gracefully as she could, her feet aching, thanks to two hours spent standing in heels. Thank God she hadn't worn the shoes Noelle had tried to foist on her—sky-high, candy-apple-red Manolo Blahniks. She'd need a wheel-chair.

She took a sip of champagne and sighed, watching the partygoers enjoy themselves. Marisa was chatting it up with a manager who had flown in from L.A. to see her perform. Ethan and Jean-Michel were schmoozing a group of investors Judith was courting for a Broadway run. She couldn't spot Nick anywhere, but Malcolm was on the dance floor, doing a fair impression of the tango with one of the ushers. Holly smiled wistfully as he dipped the young woman, making her screech and giggle.

Why couldn't she be like Malcolm and the others,

cheerful and lighthearted and apparently unconcerned about what was in store? She always got a little gloomy when a show closed, even as a techie in high school and college. Ethan called it her "postproduction depression."

But this time it was about more. This time it was about Nick.

She'd been preparing herself for this moment ever since her realization in the hospital. Four weeks of steeling her heart for the day the show would close in New Haven and, with no word yet on a Broadway transfer, he'd go back to the west coast. Keeping to her stupid "casual fun" credo. And the end result?

Epic fail.

There was nothing casual about her feelings for Nick. All she'd accomplished was to put herself on edge for what could have been four amazing weeks with the man she loved. The man she'd always love, even if he was thousands of miles and a lifestyle away from her. Some days the joy of seeing her show on stage had barely registered through her moping. Her play and her affair were over as of tonight.

Someone clinked a glass and Holly looked up to see that the band had stopped playing and the dance floor had cleared. Judith stood in the center, champagne flute in one hand, spoon in the other, surrounded by Ethan and the investors he'd been wooing.

"If I could have your attention." Someone passed Judith a microphone, which she traded for the glass. "I won't take up too much of your time. I know you all want to get back to eating, drinking and dancing. At my expense."

Laughter rippled through the crowd. When it died down, Judith continued, "We've certainly had our share of ups and downs with this production. And I want to thank each and every one of you for the faith you showed in me

by seeing it through. I think together we created something moving and beautiful, and the critics and sold-out
audiences agreed."

Applause broke out and someone yelled, "Hear! Hear!"

"Some shows you wish would go on forever," Judith
said when the clapping faded. "*The Lesser Vessel* is definitely one of them, which is why I'm thrilled to announce
that, thanks to these fine folks from the Churchill Foundation—" she gestured to the group of dark-suited men
and women standing behind her "—this show will go on.
On Broadway, that is. This fall."

If the cheering was loud before, now it was a deafen-
ing roar. Holly, suddenly discovered in her corner and
swamped with well-wishers, sat stunned.

She'd made it. Broadway was hers again. So why did
she feel so empty?

She stood to accept their congratulations, her eyes scanning the ballroom for the one person she wanted—no,
needed—to share her success with.

"Has anyone seen Nick?"

"About five minutes ago," Jimmie Lee offered. "He was
with his agent in the bar."

"Thanks."

Holly made her way through the boisterous crowd, out
the ballroom's ornate double doors and into the lobby. Her
heels tapped briskly on the parquet floor as she hurried
past the reception desk and down the hall toward the bar.

The show was going to Broadway.

What did that mean for her and Nick? If he stayed with
the show and in New York for a few months, maybe they
had a shot at something. Something strong enough to with-
stand distance and starlets and paparazzi when he went
back to making movies.

From day one, everything about their romance had been

surreal, from finding him in the audition room for the first
time in years to falling in love. Ending their fling now
would hurt but make sense. She was braced for the sting
and could keep her dignity intact. But if they agreed to go
further and he lost interest or moved on… She had no idea
how she'd survive professing her love, then watching him
leave. The alternative—chin up, play it safe—hurt almost
as much. What was she supposed to do?

Be bold. Be brave.

Nick's advice to Mr. Traver's drama students—her own
teenage words—echoed in her mind. You didn't win without taking chances. If he'd taught her anything, it was not
to stay silent and hidden. However he reacted, she had to
know. Her body gave a little stage-fright shudder and she
checked her voice. Throat closed, vocal cords paralyzed.
Big moment coming up.

Holly heaved in a gulp of air, pushed open the door
to the bar and blinked, her vision adjusting to the mood
lighting. When she could see, she took a few steps inside,
searching for Nick. The place was a virtual ghost town,
only a couple of patrons at the far end of the bar, and neither Nick nor his agent were anywhere in sight.

She was about to head back to the party, hoping Nick
had done the same, when she heard what sounded like
Garrett's voice from a booth in the corner.

"You did it, man."

"No, we did it. I'd still be doing deodorant commercials
if it wasn't for you." The deep rumble of Nick's voice, the
clink of glasses, then silence as the two men drank.

She started toward them, wondering if they'd heard
about Judith's announcement or were just toasting the end
of a successful run at the Rep. "They want you back in
L.A. on Wednesday for costume fittings. Location shooting starts in three weeks in Indiana."

"Indiana?"

Holly froze, listening to Garrett.

"Yeah, they're doing all the baseball scenes at an old stadium in Evansville. Same one they used in *A League of Their Own.*"

"Fine by me." Nick sounded almost giddy. "Hell, I'd go to Detroit to work with Spielberg."

"Here's to you, Joe DiMaggio." They clinked glasses again. "Now let's get back to the party and celebrate. But not too much. By noon tomorrow, I need you packed and on a plane home."

"YOU OKAY?" NICK asked Holly a few hours later when they were finally alone in his apartment—the last time they'd be alone together. "You've been awfully quiet tonight. Especially for a woman who should be on top of the world." He brushed a fingertip down her arm, leaving goose bumps in its wake. "You made it, baby. The show's back on Broadway."

"I'm fine," she lied, flopping onto the couch, removing one of her shoes and wiggling her toes to make sure they still worked. She'd wanted to know how Nick felt and now she did. He was leaving the show. Leaving her. He wasn't thinking next month or even next week. More like *it's been fun, gotta run.* "Just a little overwhelmed."

"Good." He sat down next to her, taking her feet onto his lap and removing her other shoe. "Because there's something we need to talk about." His thumbs drew gentle circles along her arches, turning her bones to Jell-O.

Here it comes, she thought. *The Dear Jane speech. It's not you, it's me. We always knew this was temporary. Our lives are just too different.*

"Spielberg wants me back in L.A. as soon as possible.

I'm playing Joe DiMaggio in his new biopic. Filming starts in a few weeks."

"Oh, Nick. That's wonderful." She sat up, trying to look surprised. "I'm happy for you. Really, I am. It's the kind of film role you've always wanted. You've worked so hard. Don't worry about the show. Ethan and Judith will work their magic and find someone almost as fabulous as you for New York."

"I don't doubt that. Actors are a dime a dozen. But it's not the show I'm worried about. It's you." He massaged her toes gently. "It's us."

She pulled her feet away and tucked them underneath her, praying she sounded more laid-back than she felt. This acting thing was hard work. "We knew going into this it was only short-term. A showmance." God, she hated that word.

"I was hoping we could renegotiate our deal." Nick laid a hand on her thigh, and heat burned through the fabric of the Oscar de la Renta sheath dress Noelle had sent her as a closing-night gift, accompanied by a note threatening bodily injury if she didn't wear it to the party along with the masochistic Manolos that were back in Holly's closet. "I want to keep things going. There's Skype, email, texting. And you can come visit me on set in your downtime."

"I don't know...." It sounded good in theory. But Holly didn't have to be a fortune-teller to figure out what would happen. They'd keep up the pretense for a while. Long, steamy video-chat sessions. Heartfelt emails. Sexts. Maybe even a visit or two. Then gradually, almost imperceptibly, the messages would slow. They'd be too busy with their respective careers to see each other. And eventually their contact would stop altogether.

The poets had it all wrong. Absence didn't make the heart grow fonder. It made the heart forget.

"Don't say anything yet." He shushed her with a finger to her lips, then used it to trace their outline. "Just think of the possibilities. We're filming the baseball scenes in Evansville. And you know what they say about Indiana."

"No." She shuddered as his finger moved down her neck, following the low-cut line of her dress to the valley between her breasts. "What?"

He leaned in, his voice a warm murmur against her ear. "Indiana is for lovers."

"I'm pretty sure that's Virginia."

"Virginia, Indiana. It's all the same to me." The hand on her leg slid beneath the hem of her dress. "I'd be hot for you in Siberia."

She sighed and curved into his touch, as helpless to resist him now as she had been at sixteen. Even more so, now that she knew firsthand the heights he could bring her to in oh-so-many wicked ways she never could have imagined as a teenager. "We are pretty combustible, aren't we?"

"Downright explosive."

His lips met hers, but the kiss they shared belied their words. Tender, coaxing and sweet, it was more like a slow-burning ember than a flash fire. Tears pricked at her eyelids. Saying goodbye to him now was going to be agony. Prolonging the torture by stringing things out long-distance would just about kill her.

"You're crying," Nick said when he lifted his head.

She smiled through the stabbing pain in her heart. "They're happy tears."

He kissed one away. "Happy?"

"For you. For tonight. For this." She framed his face with her hands and kissed him, harder this time, more insistent. Desperate.

"Slow down, sugar." He freed himself from her grasp,

stood and extended his hand, pulling her up with him when she took it. "We've got all night."

"Yes." Hand in hand, she followed him to the bedroom. "We do."

They undressed each other slowly, savoring every breath, every whispered endearment, every touch. Naked, they lay on the bed, his long, broad body somehow fitting perfectly with her smaller, softer one. She hooked one leg over his hip, pulling him even closer. She wanted to inhale him, consume him, take him inside her and make him a part of her so he'd be with her always.

But Nick had other ideas. He teased her with his wicked hands and tongue on every inch of her body, from her earlobes to the sensitive skin behind her knees until she nearly wept with desire.

"Nick," she panted when she couldn't stand it one second longer. "Now."

He answered her with a long, slow thrust, entering her for what she knew would be the last time. Claiming her, as if she hadn't been his from the moment he'd resurfaced in her life.

"I need you," he said when he was fully embedded in her body. "So much."

Need. A step above want. But not quite love.

She arched her neck to run a string of kisses along his stubbled jaw. "You've got me."

He thrust again and she met him movement for movement, moan for moan, until together they exploded in a heated rush.

"Stay," he murmured as he drifted into sleep, still buried inside her.

She nodded, not able to voice the lie, and laid her head on his chest, listening to the steady sound of his breathing and the patter of raindrops on the roof. She didn't know when it had started to rain, but it suited her mood. Dreary. Hopeless. Alone.

After a few minutes, when she was sure Nick was asleep, Holly eased herself out of his embrace and out of bed, gathered her clothes and dressed quickly and quietly in the darkened bedroom, checking periodically to make sure he hadn't stirred. A strange sense of déjà vu came over her. She was running away again, chickening out the way she had that night at the Plaza. She'd never thought of herself as a quitter. But quitting Nick seemed like the only sane thing to do. He had his career to consider. And she had her heart to protect.

As she let herself out, holding the door to make sure it didn't slam shut, she consoled herself with the thought that at least this time she'd had the guts to leave him a note.

Three words.

I'm sorry. Holly.

21

"Cut." With a shake of his head, the director—Spielberg's latest golden boy—hopped out of his chair, rubbing the back of his neck and scowling at Nick, who'd flubbed his line for the umpteenth time that morning. "Why don't we break for lunch. We'll start fresh in an hour."

Nick swore under his breath and threw down the baseball bat he'd been swinging. True to character, the preteen playing the batboy stepped in and picked it up.

"Thanks." Nick gave the boy an embarrassed smile. Christ. He was becoming as obnoxious as Malcolm. "Sorry. I shouldn't have done that. I let my temper get the best of me."

"No sweat, Mr. Damone. My dad says everyone's entitled to a bad day once in a while." The boy leaned the bat against the backstop and bounded off for the craft service table.

Nick steered away from the crowded buffet toward his trailer, needing solitude more than food. The kid's dad was right. An occasional bad day was par for the course. But Nick's bad days were becoming a regular occurrence. Not even three weeks on set, and his legendary focus had deserted him. He was screwing up left and right, forgetting lines and missing his mark. He couldn't for the life of him figure out why.

Okay, that was a bald-faced lie. He knew why. He just didn't want to admit it.

Holly.

He missed her. And not the sex. Or not just the sex. He missed her laugh. Missed sitting on the lumpy sofa in his temporary apartment after rehearsal with her curled up next to him, going over the events of the day. Hell, he was even jonesing for stuff like the fruity smell of her shampoo and the adorable way her tongue poked out one corner of her mouth when she was concentrating on something extra-hard.

He barely ate. Slept like shit. Yesterday, the director had flat out asked him if he had a drug problem. He was one screwup away from getting fired.

With a groan, Nick settled onto the overstuffed couch that occupied most of the living room of the Airstream the studio had provided for him. In what had become a daily ritual, he sat down with his tablet and surfed through several theater message boards and chat rooms, looking for news of the play. Pathetic, he knew. But it was his only way of keeping track of Holly, since she'd refused to return any of his phone calls or text messages. Her family and friends hadn't been any better. They were harder to crack than Fort Knox. Devin had even threatened to tie him down and tattoo his ass if he kept—in her words—"blowing up her phone."

He was on one of the most popular—and poisonous—boards, *Broadway Buzz,* when he struck gold. The subject line alone was enough to make him lose his lunch, if he'd eaten any: **Newbie playwright a prima donna? Holly Ryan storms out of auditions**.

"Shit." He clicked on the link, which led him to a blurb in the *New York Post*'s infamous gossip column, Page Six:

Still reeling from the arrest of one of its producers, Ted Aaronson, *The Lesser Vessel,* the domestic-violence drama slated to open at the Lyceum in October, may have a new problem child to deal with—fledgling playwright Holly Ryan. According to eyewitnesses, Ryan stormed out of recent auditions to replace Nick Damone, best known for his screen portrayal of action hero Trent Savage, who left the production to take the title role in Steven Spielberg's *Joltin' Joe,* based on the life of legendary Yankees slugger Joe DiMaggio. No word on the reason for Ryan's outburst, but sources close to the show say she and Damone were "quite the couple" in New Haven, where the show had a successful out-of-town tryout.

Nick shut down his tablet and reached for his cell. He'd blow up Devin's phone, Ethan's, Gabe's—heck, even Holly's parents'—but he was going to get some answers from someone. The Holly described in here wasn't the Holly he knew. He needed to know what had happened. And why.

Four phone calls later, Nick finally heard a live voice on the other end of the line.

"Hallo?"

Crap. For some reason, he'd expected Holly's mother to answer the phone at the nursery, not her father. The longest conversation Nick had had with him had lasted all of two minutes and involved flowering hibiscus.

"Um, hi, Mr. Nelson. This is Nick. Nick Damone. Holly's, uh, friend. From the play." Great. He sounded like a complete idiot.

"Of course, Niklas. Holly's not here. She's in New York."

"I know. I just… I was hoping… I wondered if you'd seen or spoken to her lately."

"I talked to her yesterday."

"Did she seem okay to you? Was she angry or upset?"

"You read the article in the *Post,* I take it?"

"Yes, sir." There was something about Nils Nelson's old-world manners, even long-distance, that made Nick slip into formality.

"Why not call her yourself and ask?"

"I would, but she won't take my calls."

"Ah," Nils said after a moment. "A lovers' spat."

"It's not that. We weren't… I mean, I'm not…"

"Aren't you?" Nils's voice was soft but pointed. "Let me ask you this, Niklas. Why do you think Holly walked out of auditions?"

"So she did walk out. I hoped it was an exaggeration."

"Unfortunately, no."

Nick rubbed his forehead. "I can't imagine why Holly would do something like that."

"Can't you?"

"She's never anything less than professional when it comes to her work."

"And you, Niklas. Are you anything less than professional when it comes to your work?"

"Usually," Nick blurted out without thinking. "But lately…" He trailed off, remembering his flubbed lines, missed marks and temper tantrums.

"Lately?"

"I've been distracted."

"As has Holly. For much the same reason as you, I think."

There was an awkward silence while Nick rolled Nils's words around in his mind. Was Holly as miserable as he was? Then why hadn't she wanted to keep things going? Why had she run out on him?

"Do you love her?" Nils asked finally, breaking the stillness.

"I think so," Nick answered, for the first time voicing what had been growing inside him for months. He wasn't his father. Holly wasn't his mother. And what they had together was a hell of a lot more than a showmance. What they had was love. The once-in-a-lifetime kind. The kind men fought wars, slayed dragons—gave up Spielberg films—for.

Now all he had to do was prove it to her.

"Be sure," Nils cautioned him. "Be very sure. When you are, you'll know what to do."

Oh, he knew what to do. He was going to New York to get his part back. And his girl.

Not necessarily in that order.

"THANKS…" HOLLY GLANCED down at the head shot on the table in front of her. "Justin. Callbacks are next week. We'll be in touch with your agent if we need to see more from you."

"Is it me?" Ethan crumpled up a piece of paper and threw it at the door as it swung shut behind the latest actor vying to fill Nick's size-thirteen shoes. "Or are they getting worse?"

"Now, now." Holly flipped Justin's head shot over and put it on top of the when-hell-freezes-over pile, which was about three times the size of the you're-not-Nick-but-we'll-give-you-another-shot pile. "I'm supposed to be the temperamental one. Remember?"

"Is that *Post* thing still bothering you?" Judith sniffed. "Everyone who was in the room that day knows what really happened."

Holly doubted that. Ethan had covered for her, falling back on the tried-and-true "family emergency" excuse. But the reality was that sleep deprivation and stress—all thanks to her breakup with Nick—had finally caught up with her. She was a loose cannon waiting to explode. All it had taken to light the ignition was an offhand remark from an actor that he'd seen the show at the Rep and would make "different choices" than Nick in the role.

At least she'd had sense enough to get out before she'd said something really embarrassing, like that no one could replace Nick. In the show or in her heart.

"I'm over it." Holly shrugged halfheartedly. "Today's another day. Who knows? Our new star could be right outside that door."

"Maybe." Ethan lifted his sleeve to check the Tag Heuer watch he'd bought himself as an opening-night gift in New Haven. "But we'll have to wait until after lunch to find out. Who's up for the Westway?"

Judith shook her head and stuffed some papers into her oversize purse. "I've got a status conference at the Churchill Foundation. But I'll be back in time for this afternoon's session."

"I'm out, too." Holly pulled her laptop from the messenger bag at her feet and put it on the table in front of her. "My agent wants a rough draft of my next play by Friday. Apparently we have to start shopping it ASAP. Can you bring me back my usual?"

"You mean that disgusting concoction of leaves and twigs you call a salad?"

"It's not disgusting."

"That's a matter of opinion." Ethan linked arms with Judith and steered her to the door. "Don't work too hard, Hollypop. Just ignore the fact that we're all counting on you to pen our next hit."

"Right." Holly said. "No pressure or anything."

Within a few minutes she was immersed in her latest script, a bittersweet tale of love, loss and liberation. Not surprising, given her tendency to follow the write-what-you-know school of thought. As she pecked at the keyboard, her muscles loosened, the pressures of the past few days forgotten. There was something about the creative process that calmed her, even when she was ripping herself open and exposing her wounds to the world.

She was deep into her story when the door squeaked open.

"Back already? You can put my salad over there." She waved her hand to indicate the opposite end of the table. "I want to finish this scene before my muse deserts me."

"Oh, I'm back, all right," a familiar voice, low and husky, drawled. "And I brought you something. But it's not a salad."

The hair at the back of her neck stood on end.

Nick?

She looked up, slowly, hesitantly, and sure enough, there he stood, lounging against the doorjamb as if he owned the place.

"What happened to the Equity monitor?" She winced. Seriously? Almost three weeks apart and those were the first words out of her mouth? Devin and Noelle would be sorely disappointed in her.

"I gave him twenty bucks and an autograph and told him to come back in half an hour." He crossed the room, rested one butt cheek on the table next to her computer and leaned in, invading her space so she could feel his breath on her cheek and smell his cologne—the same woodsy, earthy scent that she would forever associate with him. "That gives me time enough to convince you to come with me."

She closed her laptop and pushed away from the table,

trying to escape his sphere of influence. Like that was possible. "I can't go to Indiana, Nick. Or wherever you're filming now. I'm needed here."

"We're not going to the set." He pulled a key ring from the pocket of his leather jacket. "The destination I have in mind is a bit closer. And much more personal."

"Wait a minute." She tilted her head to study him, noticing for the first time the dark circles under his eyes. It looked as if she wasn't the only one having trouble sleeping. "Why aren't you on set? You're going to get fired."

"I'll explain on the way there." He jangled the keys and stood. "Come on. We're burning daylight."

"Hang on, superstar." She sat back, crossing her arms. "I'm not going anywhere with you until you tell me what's going on."

"Okay. We'll play this scene your way." He grabbed a folding chair and sat facing her, so close their knees touched, setting off a flurry of butterflies in her stomach. "I'm not on set because I'm not doing the film. I quit, Holly."

"What?" she shrieked. "You can't…"

"I can. And I did."

"Why?"

He reached over, taking her hand. "I think you know why."

"No." She shook her head and tried to pull away, but he held her hand in an iron grip. "Please tell me you didn't throw away your career for me."

"I didn't throw away my career. I chose a different one. One that lets me do the kind of work I want, when I want and with whomever I want."

"But Spielberg…"

"Isn't who I want to be with right now."

"Nick, I can't let you…"

"You're not letting me do anything. I'm doing what's best for me. Personally and professionally." He brought their entwined hands to his lips and brushed them across her knuckles. "What good's all the success in the world if you can't share it with the woman you love?"

"Love?" She stared at him, her anxiety giving way to something that felt a lot like hope.

"You haven't figured it out yet?" He massaged her hand, rubbing circles on the back with his thumb. "I'm in love with you, Holly. And you're in love with me, too."

The hope growing in her heart took root and bloomed like one of her father's prize azaleas, and her mouth curled into a smile. "Pretty sure of yourself, aren't you?"

"So sure I bought you a present." He jangled the keys again.

"Keys?"

"What the keys go to." He let go of her hand to trace a finger along her temple, tucking a loose strand of hair behind her ear. "A house. Our house."

"You bought us a house?" she squeaked.

"In Stockton. It's on a lake, with a dock where we can fish, swim…" He paused, his eyes darkening to almost black. "Make love. Of course, the pagoda will have to go."

"Oh. My. God." She drew in a deep breath then exhaled slowly. "I can't believe you bought the Paganos' house."

"It's where we began." His eyes locked onto hers. "I figured it was where we should grow old together."

"Grow old?" Her head reeled and her heart skipped what seemed like ten beats. Did he mean…?

"I want to marry you, Holly. I want to work with you and play with you and have babies with you and—"

Anything else he was going to say was lost as she cut him off, grabbing the lapels of his jacket and tugging him to her for a deep, soulful kiss. When she pulled back he had a grin as wide as the George Washington Bridge.

"I take it that means yes."

"You bet it does. Yes to everything. The work, the play, the babies." She ran her hands down his jacket to rest on his chest. "Lots of babies."

"Girls with your eyes and my hair. And boys who can play any sport they want. Or not."

A flash of disappointment crossed his face, making her frown. "You won't mind living in the same town as your father?"

"Not as long as you're there, too." His heart beat steady beneath her hand. "Besides, we'll still have the apartment at the Plaza. And my place in Malibu."

"I love you, Nick. I don't want to be without you."

"You won't be." He kissed her, quick, hard and reassuring. "There may be times our careers pull us apart temporarily, but we'll make it work. I swear."

"I know."

"So what do you say?" He stood, the keys swinging from his fingers. "Want to go home?"

"What about the auditions?"

He pulled her up, lifting her off her feet, and kissed her until she was aching and breathless. "How's that for an audition?"

"You've got the part." She clung to him, wrapping her legs around his waist. "Let's wait for Ethan and Judith so we can tell them the good news. Then I'm all yours."

"That's the best offer I've had all year." He quirked an eyebrow and smiled. Not his movie-star smile, but a slow, sultry one, especially for her. "Except I don't know what we'll do with ourselves in the meantime."

She rained kisses down his throat, breathing him in. "You're a smart guy. I'm sure you'll think of something."

And he did.

Epilogue

THE LAST TIME Holly sat in the audience at Radio City Music Hall she was eight years old, with her family in the nosebleed seats, watching the Rockettes high-kick to "We Wish You a Merry Christmas."

Now she sat in the fourth row, next to her stage- and screen-star husband, watching Neil Patrick Harris and a bevy of Broadway gypsies deliver an epic opening number at the Tony Awards.

Life. Was. Good.

"Still breathing?" Nick whispered in her ear during a commercial break about halfway through the show.

"Barely." Her hands fluttered in her lap and she clasped them together to keep them still. "Aren't you nervous? Your category's next."

"Nah." He leaned back and stretched out his arms, infuriatingly calm. "I already got my prize."

He bent his head to kiss her, soft and slow, with a familiarity that came with six months of marriage, just as the camera panned to them. The audience tittered, and a giggling actress who'd won one of last year's awards announced Nick's name as one of the nominees for best performance by a leading actor in a play.

"That'll make Neil's wrap-up rap," Nick joked when he came up for air. "I'll bet Lin Manuel Miranda's back there writing about it as we speak."

"Oh, God. Our parents just watched us make out on the Jumbotron." Holly glanced up at the balcony, where Nick's mom and her family sat, with the exception of Ivy, who was in Milan shooting the cover of Italian *Vogue*. With Nick at her side, she'd finally been able to tell them about the full extent of her ex-husband's abuse and the child she'd lost. It hadn't been easy. There had been lots of hugs, crying and swearing, the first two for Holly and the last directed at her ex. She hated seeing them hurt for her. But the news she and Nick shared with them had taken away some of the sting.

"We're married now, babe." He dropped an arm across her shoulders. "We're allowed to make out."

"And the Tony goes to…" The actress broke the seal on the envelope and paused, making Holly want to run up there and rip the damn thing out of her hand. Although she'd probably fall on her face doing it, thanks to the gold Donna Karan mermaid gown and matching Valentino sling-backs Noelle had convinced her were "a must" for a Tony nominee. She didn't want to think about how long it was going to take her to get up onstage if, by some miracle, they took home the statuette for best play.

But the sexy grin on Nick's face when she'd walked out of their bedroom that afternoon made all the primping worthwhile. They'd missed the pre-party altogether and barely made it to the ceremony in time to walk the red carpet.

After what seemed like an eternity, the actress looked up and leaned into the microphone. "Nick Damone, for *The Lesser Vessel*."

Holly squealed and Nick swept her up in a bear hug and

laid another long, wet kiss on her, no doubt to the delight of the cameras and the crowd. "I love you," he breathed into her hair.

She kissed the corner of his mouth. "Ditto."

"See you backstage."

"Only if I win, too."

"You will." He winked. "Don't forget to thank me in your acceptance speech."

Nick strode down the aisle to the stage, looking finer than fine in an Armani tux that showed off his sculpted body. He stopped periodically to shake hands, finally reaching the stage and dwarfing the diminutive actress as he accepted his Tony statuette from her.

Then he was at the microphone. Holly caught her name and heard him mention his mom, but the rest was a blur. Thank God for YouTube. Some overzealous fan would have Nick's speech uploaded within the hour. Maybe by then she'd be coherent enough to actually pay attention to it.

Then again, she thought, spotting Tom Hanks two rows in front of her yucking it up with Elton John, *maybe not.* The whole night was surreal. She'd be flying on this high for at least a week.

It was another half hour before they got around to handing out the final two awards of the night: Best Play and Best Musical. White-knuckled, Holly gripped the armrests on either side of her seat as one of the performers in last year's winning show read the nominees in the play category.

"Got your speech ready?" Ethan, who had been sitting a few rows behind her with Jean-Michel, slid into Nick's vacant seat. "Don't forget to thank me."

"Nick said the same thing."

"And the Tony goes to…"

Ethan grabbed her hand and gave her an excited smile

she was too nauseated to return. Had anyone ever thrown up at one of these things? There'd be a certain distinction in being the first. At least, that's what Holly told herself.

"The Lesser Vessel."

Holly's heart swelled. She struggled to catch her breath and hold back the tears threatening to cascade down her cheeks. It was almost too much, too good to be true. She had her family, and Nick, and his mom and now a career she loved, with the respect of her peers. And soon…

"Wake up, space cadet." Ethan jostled her shoulder. "You won."

"We won," she said, pulling him up with her. "Come on. I'm not doing this alone. Besides, I might need help on the stairs. This gown is impossible to walk in. And don't get me started on the shoes."

They made it to the stage, where they were congratulated, and Holly was handed her statuette. She fingered the silver disk, etched with the comedy and tragedy masks that symbolized the theater. "Wow." She flicked the shiny medallion, spinning it. "I guess now we have bookends."

The audience laughed, and she looked over her shoulder at Ethan, who gave her an encouraging nod. "In all seriousness, this is truly an honor. This time last year, I was eating ramen noodles and mac and cheese, struggling to get by while I wrote the play of my heart. Now I'm standing in front of you all, my peers, holding this—" she raised the statuette "—as validation that it was all worth it."

Holly took a deep breath, wiped away a tear and continued, "There're so many people I need to thank. Judith Aaronson and the Churchill Foundation for putting their money behind my words. Ethan Phelps and the entire cast and crew, for bringing them to life. My family and friends, for seeing me through some pretty dark times. And last, but no way near least, my husband, who…"

A commotion in the wings made her stop and turn. Nick, tall, dark and delicious, the stage lights bouncing off his thick, black hair, crossed the stage toward her.

She covered the microphone with one hand. "I thought you said to meet you backstage."

"I couldn't wait." The sexy grin was back, with a playful spark in his eyes to boot.

"For what?" Her hand fell away from the microphone, the crowd forgotten. All that mattered in that moment was the man—her man—standing in front of her, opening himself up before their family, friends and pretty much all of New York's theater elite in a way she never imagined possible just twelve months ago.

"For this."

To the hoots and catcalls of the audience, he scooped her up and kissed her so passionately she was sure the network censors were poised with their fingers over the red button. When he was done, he raised his head, beaming, and she pointed at the conductor in the orchestra pit.

"You can cue the music. I'm done."

Holly laughed as Nick carried her offstage to an up-tempo version of "Can't Help Lovin' Dat Man," one hand wrapped around his neck for balance, the other still clutching her Tony.

A backstage attendant sporting headphones and carrying a clipboard waved her arm, directing them up a flight of stairs.

"Where are you taking me?"

"Pressroom."

"Are you planning on carrying me there?"

"If I have to."

"Sure you can handle it?" She looked down at her stomach, still flat for the time being. "I've put on a few pounds."

"You're not even showing yet." He hefted her a little higher, as if to prove his point.

"But I will be. Soon. I'll be as big as a whale and I won't be able to see my feet and—"

"And I'll still be there to pick you up. You and this baby are everything to me."

"Oh, Nick." She tipped her head back to look at him, and her breath caught at the depth of emotion reflected in his eyes. "I'm scared. What if...?"

"Shh. It's going to be different this time. I'll do whatever it takes to make sure you're safe and comfortable." He traced her jawline with his knuckles, making her shiver. "Even if it means carting you around until you give birth."

She buried her nose in his neck, reveling in his warm male smell and the crispness of his collar against her cheek. "What did I do to deserve you?"

"I ask myself the same question about you every day." They reached the pressroom door and he paused to brush a soft kiss across her forehead. "Ready to face the fourth estate?"

She bit her lip. "What do we say when they ask what's next for us?"

He blew out a long breath and smiled. "How about we tell them we're working on something very special that we'll be ready to debut in about six months?"

"That sounds perfect." She threaded her fingers through the hair at the nape of his neck, bringing his head down to hers, and kissed him. "Absolutely perfect."

* * * * *